P9-CRX-559

6-321

michael laser

6-321

Atheneum Books for Young Readers
New York London Toronto Sydney Singapore

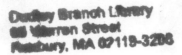
Atheneum Books for Young Readers
An imprint of Simon & Schuster Children's Publishing Division
1230 Avenue of the Americas
New York, New York 10020

Book design by Angela Carlino
The text of this book is set in Bembo.

Printed in the United States of America

10 9 8 7 6 5 4 3 2 1

Library of Congress Cataloging-in-Publication Data
Laser, Michael.
    6-321 / by Michael Laser.—1st ed.
        p. cm.
Summary: Sixth grade in a public school in Queens brings many
changes into the life of Marc Chaikin, as he falls in love, deals with
class bullies, overcomes his fear of school, and faces his parents'
divorce.
ISBN 0-689-83372-5
[1. Schools—Fiction. 2. Interpersonal relations—Fiction.
3. New York (N.Y.)—Fiction.] I. Title: Six-three two one.
II. Title.
PZ7.L32717 Aac 2001
[Fic]—dc21   99-59359

6/01

FIRST
EDITION

*To my father
and to Jennifer*

acknowledgments

Caitlin Van Dusen, my editor, cared enough about this book to stick with it through several major revisions, and gave detailed, intelligent suggestions at each step of the way. I'm deeply grateful, Caitlin.

Pamela Pollack was the first to encourage me to go ahead and write this; she then suggested changes to my first draft.

The Department of Special Collections, Milbank Memorial Library, Teachers College at Columbia University, gave me access to sixth-grade curricula in New York City's public schools, circa 1963.

The libraries of Montclair and Bloomfield,

New Jersey, and Montclair State College, and the indispensable New Jersey Nightline telephone reference service enabled me to cite the movies, TV shows, headlines, and music of the time— and even to describe the weather on a certain dramatic day in history.

And the following people answered my pleas for help with information and ideas that became part of the book: Jennifer Prost, Michelle Wong, Rachel and James Bleshman, Lucia Vassallo, and Nina Boire.

Thank you all!

6-321

chapter 1

Most years in school, not much happens. You do math problems with more and more digits, you write reports on books with more and more pages, but basically every grade is the same. Historic events like the first manned space flight might be taking place outside the school, but inside, nothing changes except how tall you and your friends are.

Sixth grade was different, though. More went on this past year than the rest of my life put together. In just two months I fell in love, watched my family break into pieces, and came this close to getting beat to a pulp along with all my friends—not to mention meeting Mickey

Mantle and getting attacked by the biggest juve-
nile delinquent in the school. When I think
back to what I was like in September, and then
compare it with now, it's like the year was a
nuclear chain reaction, exploding the scared kid
I used to be and turning me into a more grown-
up self.

Because until last September, school terrified
me. Every year I couldn't eat breakfast for the
whole first week. At our school you couldn't
even whisper without a teacher pulling you out
of line, pushing you against a wall, and yelling in
your face, "This is going on your permanent
record!" My strategy for staying out of trouble
was to keep quiet and invisible. If they didn't see
you, they couldn't pull you out, right?

The first day of sixth grade scared me worse
than ever, because my teacher was going to be
Mr. Vigoritti, the strictest, loudest-yelling teacher
in the school. With his famous bald head and
glasses, he could turn a whole auditorium quiet
just by walking in the door. You might think that
after a lifetime of hearing my parents scream at
each other, teachers raising their voices wouldn't
bother me—but it worked the opposite way. I
got paralyzed every time Mr. Vigoritti yelled at
some kid on the other side of the playground in

that voice that could cut through a sonic boom. People told legends about his hot temper—like that he once slammed his door so hard, the glass in the window broke.

But it turned out that he didn't shout so much inside his classroom, except to say, "SHATTAP" if we made too much noise. And he hardly ever slammed the door. (The few times he did, the glass never even rattled, let alone broke.) So, after a few weeks, I learned to calm down and stop being so scared.

Then I found out that I wasn't the only nervous one. One of my classmates had it even worse than I did.

Mr. Vigoritti assigned me to do a report on Pizarro, the conquistador. And Lily Wu. I had known Lily since kindergarten. She was a quiet girl with a sweet smile who worked hard and got only Excellents on her report card, but she never raised her hand in class because she was so shy.

We did our work in the public library and came up with an original idea for the report. Mr. Vigoritti loved anything different from just standing up there reading, so we decided to debate like President Kennedy did when he ran against Nixon. I would play Pizarro, and she would play the Inca king Atahualpa, the one who got conquered. We would each tell our side of the story, slipping in the facts along the way.

She concentrated hard, writing her Lily way at the library table, with her wrist curved around the top of her loose-leaf so she wrote upward instead of across. If I found a funny or gruesome fact, like that the Incas predicted the future from animal guts, I would read it to her in a whisper, and she would either laugh or go, "Uchh." We were so comfortable with each other back then— it's amazing to me, considering what happened later.

She lived across from me, on the opposite side of the ball field. The morning of the report, I ran into her on the way to school. She looked sick, so I asked if she was okay. At first she said yes, but then she admitted, "I'm nervous about the report."

That caught me by surprise. She was the smartest girl in the class—she wrote a forty-page report on the social, economic, and political history of Queens that Mr. Vigoritti typed up himself and mailed to the borough president's office, which sent back a letter of commendation. What did she have to worry about?

"It's no big deal," I said, to reassure her. "We have the whole thing written down."

"I know, but I hate getting up in front of everybody. I wish he would let us just hand it in."

To make it easier on her, I said, "Are you kidding? The whole *idea* of school is to scare you. Did you think it was to learn things? Ha! It's to keep you petrified out of your wits so you'll just sit there and shut up."

Her laugh sounded like a bubble popping. She gave me a grateful smile, like she was glad to have me for a friend, and that smile hit me like a lightning bolt. We had known each other so long that I had never paid much attention to her before. But now I saw her completely clearly, like she had just floated down to Earth in a beam of light.

She was beautiful. She had dark, sad eyes and shiny black hair. Her bangs ended in a straight line in the middle of her forehead, and her ears were shaped perfectly. Even the round, white collar of her blouse seemed cleaner and more modest than anyone else's.

That's when it all started, right between the garages and the big Dumpster: the feeling that no one in the world was as beautiful and nice as Lily, and no one else could appreciate her the way I did. But how could she feel the same way about me when I was just an average student with nothing to make me stand out?

That one moment changed everything. Before I noticed Lily, I was the kind of kid who built model cars and played ball and went rock-hunting, never thinking too much about anything. Once she got into my mind, though, I started *always* thinking—about what I should say to her, or how it would be if we got married someday, or how I wished we could walk down the turnpike together, past all the stores, with her holding my hand and smiling that same smile at me.

During our report, she kept her eyes down on the pages, which shook a little because her hands were trembling. Her voice had a nervous quiver, too, as she explained how the Inca empire was a great civilization that had made a mountainous region fertile with terrace farming and irrigation, that had built temples from huge stones that fit so perfectly, they didn't need cement. I wanted to hold both of her hands and tell her, "Don't worry, you're doing great." The more nervous she got, the more I wished I could hug her.

I had planned to ham it up as Pizarro, acting like a tough guy, "These Incas were savages before we came, they had no system of writing, they used to sacrifice humans to the gods! You call that civilization, *Mis*ter Atahualpa?" But when my turn came, I just read my script and tripped over my tongue a couple times, because I was worrying about Lily's opinion of me instead of concentrating on the words.

Mr. Vigoritti taught us later about the word "irony." Here's a good example: the minute I noticed Lily, that same minute I stopped knowing how to talk to her. Which made the next couple months a kind of torture.

In the playground after lunch, I stayed by myself at the fence so I could peek at her and feel that achy feeling. I had my fingers through the metal links and pretended to be looking at the big mental hospital across the field. Nicky Raffetto, the school delinquent, was showing off how his friends could bang into his shoulder but couldn't knock him over. Lily and her friend Julie Oshinsky were playing cat's cradle underneath one of the basketball backboards. Lily looked so small and delicate next to Julie, who is a great person and lots of fun but seemed kind of husky by comparison. I wished I could hear them, in case Lily was talking about me.

A hoarse, mocking laugh came from behind

me, and I recognized it as Cary Lipshitz's laugh. He was the leader of the cool, tall boys, but a pretty nasty and sarcastic person. Is he laughing at me? I wondered. Can he tell I like Lily? Then, before I knew what was happening, someone knocked me off my feet, and I had gravel grinding into my face. What the——?! Over my shoulder I saw Nicky Raffetto sitting on my back and punching me in the ribs, with his face in a rage. He wasn't any bigger than me, but he had turned into a mad dog and I didn't even know what was going on, so he had the advantage. I tried to throw him off, but he held on tight and kept socking me in the back, saying, "You think *that's* funny?"

Before I could do anything except say, "Get off me!" Mr. Vigoritti's voice boomed across the playground: "Nicholas Raffetto! Get against the fence, NOW!"

Nicky didn't listen, though. He didn't stop hitting me until he was yanked off. Mr. Vigoritti helped me up onto my feet. "Explain to me," he roared at Nicky, "why you had to hit this boy. Was it an uncontrollable urge? You just *had* to attack someone who wasn't bothering you?"

Nicky didn't answer, he just looked down at his shoes. To him, teachers were like cops to a criminal: the Enemy. He wouldn't give them the satisfaction of talking.

I had black grit on my white shirt, I was all scraped, plus everyone I knew had seen me getting creamed (especially Lily), but at least Mr. Vigoritti saw what happened, so I wasn't in trouble. That's what I thought, anyway—until I heard the footsteps. Those wooden heels on the hard pavement, *tick-tock tick-tock,* like a fast clock telling you it's time for the electric chair.

Mr. Eisenman. The principal.

Mr. Vigoritti explained what had happened, but the principal didn't care who was right and who was wrong. He just stood there with his thick red hair and angry eyes like bullets. He wanted P.S. 260 to be the best school in Queens, and to him that meant a thousand students sitting with their hands folded on their desks and their hair combed, not moving, not talking, not even blinking. Only a maniac (or Nicky Raffetto) would dare to fight in the school yard with Mr. Eisenman around.

When Mr. Vigoritti finished explaining, the principal ignored what he had said and asked Nicky and me in his hard-as-steel robot voice, "Do you know what 'barbarian' means?"

It didn't seem like a question we were supposed to answer, so we didn't. Then he turned his furious eyes on just me. "Do you condone fighting in the school yard?"

I couldn't talk. My throat wouldn't open up. Except for getting pulled out once in fourth grade for whispering in the hall, no teacher had ever caught me doing anything against the rules, so I had managed to escape getting yelled at the way Nicky and his friends always did. I didn't think I could survive that kind of treatment—but now the principal had me in his sights, and there was no place to hide.

Mr. Vigoritti stood up for me one more time. "This boy is a good student. I've never had a problem with him. He did absolutely nothing to provoke this fight."

(In the middle of my fear, I couldn't help being surprised. I never knew he'd even noticed me!)

Unfortunately the principal didn't care what Mr. Vigoritti said. He asked Nicky the same question as me. "Do *you* condone fighting in the school yard?"

If I didn't know what "condone" meant, then Nicky sure didn't. He looked down at his shoes again, but Mr. Eisenman lifted his chin up and held it there. "Don't look away when someone is talking to you," he ordered. So Nicky looked him in the eye, but still didn't answer.

"There will be no fighting in this school yard," Mr. Eisenman said. "I will not tolerate uncouth behavior or disturbance of the peace. And I will not listen to excuses."

Then he had our shoulders locked in his bear-trap hands and was hauling us away, into the building and down the long, dark corridor, like an ogre dragging his next meal back to his cave.

Instead of eating us, he took us to Mrs. Marx's classroom. She was my first-grade teacher, but she didn't seem to recognize me. The principal told us to go sit at the round table in the back of the room, on those chairs for little kids, while he whispered to her. Then he came and stood over us. He said, "Since you obviously haven't learned about civilized behavior, you'll have to start over from the beginning."

The first graders all turned in their chairs to watch us. We must have looked as big as high school students to them. I controlled myself, trying hard not to show how scared and upset I was. They couldn't really make us go through school again from first grade up—could they? Part of me wanted to cry, especially when the principal left and the class went back to singing kiddy songs along with a phonograph record.

For a long time Nicky and I just stared at the table. Mrs. Marx gave us a sour look over her glasses every once in a while, but otherwise she ignored us. Could they really put you back into first grade? It didn't seem legal. On the other hand, the principal was like the captain of a ship: he could do anything he wanted, as long as he didn't kill us or break any bones.

The ridiculous part was that I didn't even know why Nicky had attacked me. I figured it must have been part of the feud between my class and his class, which had been building up since about third grade. The bigger, heavier boys in Nicky's class had always hated the smart little skinny guys in my class, just like the classes in the years before us. Two or three of them used to wait behind a bush now and then to attack one of us, just for fun. But in sixth grade we started fighting back, and that turned it from bullying into an all-out war. I can't explain *why* we had the feud. It must have been some kind of animal instinct, like cats and birds. A day or two before the incident with Nicky, Scott Siegel, the shortest kid in our class, had gotten beat up in the parking lot behind the stores, coming home with a bag of bagels, so I guessed today was my turn.

I wanted to say to Nicky, "You are such a stupid idiot, knocking me down when I never did anything to you"—but he seemed so tough and dangerous, with hair that swooped down over his forehead instead of being crew cut like everyone else's, I couldn't imagine even talking to him.

While the first graders were singing their songs, someone burped and the whole class giggled. Mrs. Marx scolded them by saying, like the Queen of England, "I cahn't *stahhhhhnd* immaturity"—to a bunch of six-year-olds! Nicky mumbled, "Damn fool." Then, when the kids were singing again, he added, "Look at her old dried-out elbows. They ought to take her and shoot her."

I couldn't help letting out a "Ha!" Mrs. Marx gave us another over-the-glasses look and warned us, "Boys," but after a while we both started muttering insults back and forth about the babyish songs and her dumpy, lumpy dress. "Looks like a sack of potatoes," I said. Nicky said he couldn't wait to get out of this garbage can of a school. If he got left back, he'd set fire to the building. In junior high they left you alone, he said. You could even smoke in the school yard as long as you did it in the corner and kept your back turned.

He acted like he was talking to himself, not me, and I did the same thing. You wouldn't call it a friendly conversation, but you wouldn't think we had just been wrestling on the pavement, either.

Toward the end of the day, while Mrs. Marx read the class a story, I finally came out and whispered, "Next time you jump on me, wait till we're not in school, okay?"

He shook his head like *No can do,* and muttered, "Nobody laughs at me and gets away with it."

I told him I hadn't laughed at him. Then I remembered that hoarse laugh behind me— Cary Lipshitz. "That was someone else," I said.

He stared at my face to see if I was lying. When I didn't look away, he knew he had made a mistake, but instead of apologizing, he just shrugged.

So there I was, beat up in front of Lily and put back to first grade, all because Cary Lipshitz had laughed at Nicky Raffetto. It was so unfair that I couldn't do anything but shake my head.

When three o'clock came and nobody rescued us, I started worrying that Mr. Eisenman really meant it, that he would force us to go through grammar school all over again. It was like getting dragged to the bottom of the ocean by an iron ball. How could I tell my parents? They had been arguing worse than ever lately, getting into scary rages, like when my mother threw a high-heel shoe at my father's face. If I had to break this news about getting put back to first grade, my mother would probably sob and shriek, and my father (who worked so much, I hardly ever saw him) would spend the weekends screaming at me, "You ruined your life!"

Before I passed out from fear, Mrs. Marx came to our table and told us we could go back to our regular classrooms the next day. "I hope you've learned a lesson from this," she warned.

I did. I learned that even if the thing I was most afraid of happened, even if Mr. Eisenman stared me in the face and threatened to crush me, I would still survive. I learned that he was a mean bully but also a lying fake, and I had been terrified all these years for nothing.

Outside the school Nicky and I joined up with our friends. He went with his, down the hill to the Italian neighborhood, and I went with mine, across the street to the garden apartments where most of us lived.

Everyone wanted to know what Mr. Eisenman did to us. I told them the whole story, including how full of it he was. They were more interested in Nicky, though. They called him a psycho and said he'd probably go on a killing spree someday and get life plus ninety-nine years.

I said, "I don't know. He's tough, but he's not crazy."

They looked at me like I was brainwashed.

chapter 2

About a week after that, the principal put Nicky in our class. He had lit a mat of firecrackers in the school yard after three o'clock, thinking (incorrectly) the teachers would all be gone. The principal figured that only a man could discipline him, and Mr. Vigoritti was the only male teacher in the school. So, in spite of not being able to keep up with the work, Nicky spent the rest of sixth grade with us.

You had to feel bad for him. Here he was, a guy with his own gang of followers, stuck in the middle of thirty-one people who thought to themselves, This guy is *dumb,* every time he opened his mouth. At three o'clock he still walked home like a king in the middle of his friends, spitting on the sidewalk, but in class he never opened his mouth unless Mr. Vigoritti called on him. He not only didn't get the answers right, he couldn't even pronounce half the words. One time we were going around the room reading aloud from our science book, and he pronounced hereditary "here, dittery." Cary made wisecracks about him all day long from the back of the room. Like when Nicky couldn't name the president of France, which we had learned the day before, Cary muttered, "And he's the smartest one in 6–7." (The school changed the names of all the classes a few years ago by naming them after their classrooms instead of after their rank, so the people in 6–7 wouldn't have their feelings hurt by everyone knowing they were the bottom class. But we all knew that 6–321 was really the top class, 6–1, and that 6–309 was really the bottom class, 6–7, and sometimes we still called their class that, just to insult them.) Nicky turned around and gave Cary a look like a rifle shot between the eyes. It turned out that Mr. Vigoritti heard it, too, and he said in a furious voice, "Cary, unless you're God, you don't know everything either. Your disrespect is intolerable. *GO STAND IN THE HALL.*"

Cary went, but his above-it-all grin never changed. That was why the cool boys followed him—because teachers didn't scare him. His parents must have raised him to believe he was better than everyone else, like a prince forced to live among the common folk. Although I couldn't stand him, I wished I had just a small percentage of his self-confidence.

(The best part of the story, though, was when Mr. Vigoritti called on Lily's friend Julie next, and she didn't remember that the president of France was de Gaulle either, so she answered, "Pepe Le Pew?"—the cartoon skunk. Even Mr. Vigoritti couldn't stop himself from cracking up along with the rest of us.)

Just after Nicky joined our class, two guys from 6-7 beat up Joseph Aptowitz, the genius, and took his silver pen. Some people had a theory that Nicky ordered them to do it, as revenge against Cary's insults, but I disagreed. First, those guys were *always* ganging up on us. And second, Nicky was definitely the fight-your-own-battles type. Besides, if he took revenge, it would be against Cary, not Joseph. Which left us with the mystery of why Nicky didn't just wait for Cary after school and sock him in the guts.

We found out why a few days later. On a class trip, we went to the Morris-Jumel Mansion, which is the oldest house in Manhattan—and probably the most boring. Nicky had to sit next to Mr. Vigoritti in the front seat of the bus so he wouldn't get in trouble. When it was time to go home, though, Charles Grinsberg threw up on himself and Mr. Vigoritti took him to the restroom to clean him up. The class waited on the bus, and we started rehashing the World Series. Cary was a big Yankees fan, and he never let us Mets fans forget that we had finished in last place, so various people gave it to him good about his supposedly unbeatable Bombers. Cary defended his team by saying, "If Mantle hadn't broken his foot, the whole Series would have turned out differently." Out of nowhere, Nicky answered, "That's bull and you know it." Cary snorted and said, "The voice of authority," and then Nicky turned and stared at him down the bus aisle. Even though the class mothers were on the bus, Nicky said, "Eisenman says he'll expel me the next time I fight. But I'll be waiting for you on the last day of school. You just get ready."

Cary snickered and said, "Okay, I'll learn judo." He didn't look too concerned, but—what an amazing coincidence!—he stopped making wisecracks about Nicky after that.

To help Nicky at least not get an Unsatisfactory in every subject, Mr. Vigoritti asked Lily to tutor him after school for extra credit. Every day, when the rest of us left at three o'clock, the two of them moved to the table at the back of the room. I had to come back once because I left my loose-leaf in my desk, and I saw how the tutoring was going. While Mr. Vigoritti worked on his papers up front, Lily pointed at a math problem, not even looking at Nicky, who just slouched and sneered. She had a look of agony on her face. How could Mr. Vigoritti ask such a shy girl to tutor a deliquent who didn't want her help, who didn't care what marks he got? I wanted to ask him to pick someone else to help Nicky, but then I would be exposed as liking her, so I kept my mouth shut.

The worst part was that Lily got teased because of tutoring him. Boys would sneak up behind her and say this stupid chant, "Nicky and Lily . . . woooooo," because her last name was Wu.

Each time, her face would squeeze down in pain as if someone had jabbed her with a needle. When I heard my best friend Howard do the chant, I snapped at him, "Shut up." He gave me a funny look like, What's wrong with *you?* I said, "You're hurting her feelings," and prayed he wouldn't get suspicious.

While Nicky got everything wrong and Lily got all of her tests on the 100 Club bulletin board, I had my own problems. For the first month and a half, I found a different criticism on my homework every day, like "Read between the lines," or, "Explain your reasoning," or, "You *must* improve your penmanship." Every single sheet of paper we handed in had to have a heading like this:

P.S. 260 Queens   *Marc Chaikin*
Class 6-321   *September 14, 1963*

For some reason it took me a while before I could get every part exactly right. Mr. Vigoritti turned out to be not so much the yelling type— he preferred to put us in line with a witty remark, like when people crammed into the wardrobes to get their coats, he would shake his head and say, "Piggies at the trough"—but he had extremely high standards. He called on people by going through a set of cards with our names on them (you couldn't know when you were due, because he shuffled them every day), and my name always seemed to come up during the most impossible questions. I mumbled, "I don't know" about once a day, which didn't exactly help me impress Lily. Then he would try to coax the answer out of me with hints, but I couldn't think straight under pressure, and he would have to give up and ask someone else. I didn't think I would ever satisfy him.

But in spite of his thinking my work stunk, I knew Mr. Vigoritti was the best teacher I ever had. For one thing, he used words no one knew, and made a game of us figuring out what they meant—like saying someone looked "saturnine" today, or asking someone else if he was a "philatelist." In social studies he used to write an essay on the board and leave a lot of blanks, and we had to try to fill in the words. Sometimes a blank would stump everyone, like in the essay about the president trying to raise the standard of living in Latin America, there was a sentence about an important conference held at Punta del ___, and no one knew the answer. Finally Cary raised his hand and said, "Punta del Football?" Mr. Vigoritti smiled and made a check mark in the air with his finger. And in current events, sometimes he would stop everything to explain what was behind the news—like, when we were talking about the nuclear test ban, he told us how the Cold War was worse than any conflict in history because now everyone on the planet had to live with the threat that the United States or Russia would use the atom bomb and start a nuclear war. Even children had to live under a cloud of fear, and that was a tragedy.

My favorite times, though, were the days when we had a few extra minutes before three o'clock, and he would sit on the front edge of his desk and tell us about President Kennedy. The best story was the one about the boy who asked J. F. K. how he became a war hero, and he answered, "It was involuntary. They sank my boat." Mr. Vigoritti told us about the president's ideals of liberty (he wanted to free oppressed people around the world) and courage (he wrote a book about politicians who stood up against what everybody else thought, which was the bravest and hardest thing you could do, according to J. F. K.). I would sit and look at his picture above the blackboard and imagine him with his beautiful wife, and he seemed as far above everyone I knew as a star in the sky. Whatever lousy things might happen in our school or at home, having him as our president made me proud.

One day, I found a word in the margin of my homework that I hadn't seen before: "Good." I looked around the classroom happily, wishing I could show it to Howard, but he sat three rows away. Then Mr. Vigoritti assigned us to write a review of a TV show, and I wrote one on *The Beverly Hillbillies,* which me and my friends couldn't stand even though it was the number one show in America. I wrote, "This moronic excuse for entertainment would insult the intelligence of baboons if it was shown in the zoo." He commented across the top in big letters, "Brilliant! Read to class!" So I did, and everyone laughed, and it was my greatest moment ever in school.

Although Mr. Vigoritti didn't let a single mistake get by without a mark from his fountain pen, he also made a big deal of it when you did something right. All through September I had worked hard just to escape from his criticisms, but after that "Brilliant!" I worked even harder, trying to earn more compliments. From being an average student or worse, I worked my way up into the top handful of the class—all thanks to Mr. Vigoritti's praise.

But I also spent a lot of each day gazing across the room at Lily. Mr. Vigoritti caught me once and said, "Marc, the blackboard is this way."

Whenever I saw her, it was like a rope flew to her from out of my chest and tugged on me with an ache. I remember one time especially, when we were outside in the school garden planting tulips and crocuses, so we could see them pop up in the spring and get an appreciation of nature. They gave everybody one bulb to plant, but we had to take turns with the trowels. I watched Lily kneel down with her knees close together and then dig her hole and pat the dirt slowly with the trowel, never getting her hands or her knees dirty. The year before, I remembered her laughing and smiling when we were out in the garden, but this time she looked like she wished she could be somewhere else, far away. I wanted to take her and lead her out of there, through the big gate in the fence, and make her be happy again.

The more days and weeks I watched her, the more perfect she seemed—and the harder it was to imagine her liking me. Maybe it wasn't even possible, I thought. What if her parents wouldn't let her go out with someone who wasn't Chinese? But then I remembered her friendly, skinny father calling me "Marco Polo" when I used to go over to visit. The problem wasn't her parents, it was that she was such an angel, and I was just ... me.

Usually when I came home from school, my mother sat with me in the kitchen while I had my apple and glass of milk, and she listened while I told her about anything interesting that had happened that day. One particular afternoon, though, I found my father home sick and my mother out shopping at the supermarket. He was lying on the couch in his boxer shorts and watching TV, blowing his nose and filling up a grocery bag with used Kleenexes. I sat down next to him and started sticking reinforcements on the broken holes in my loose-leaf paper while we watched *To Tell the Truth*. We never got to spend that much time together, so I always took advantage of any opportunity to be with him. Watching TV was one of the best ways because, unlike when we practiced baseball on the weekends, he couldn't yell at me for missing grounders.

As soon as my mother came home, she started screaming at him for forgetting to start the laundry. His voice changed instantly into his mean tone. "I'm sick one day in three years and you can't let me rest?"

She dropped a bag of groceries onto the counter and shrieked, "I can't do everything. I'm only one person—I can't live like this!" And he yelled back, "Stop complaining! I don't want to hear it! Just shut up!"

I felt sick to my stomach and paralyzed by the bullets flying over my head. I wanted to curl up and die, and I hated him for yelling the way he did. I also hated her for driving him crazy with housework and then getting so hysterical when they fought. I once overheard my aunt Charlotte telling her daughter that my parents had spent too many years wanting opposite things—he wanted to be free of all responsibilities, while she wanted to be loved like in a romantic movie—but explanations didn't help once the yelling started. I couldn't even go hide in my room with a pillow over my head, because then they would notice me walking away. Instead, I just stared down into my little blue box of reinforcements, thinking, They look like Life Savers, but they're not.

Do you see why I couldn't imagine someone as perfect as Lily wanting to be with me, when I came from a family like that?

The achy feeling got worse and worse, like a fatal disease. Usually I'm not the type who blabs my personal business, but it finally burst out of me.

My friend Howard and I were rock-hunting after school on Halloween, since we were too old to go trick or treating. (Some private houses had gotten built on the top of Suicide Hill a few years ago, and the digging had brought the insides of the Earth up to the surface—you can still find amazing rocks and minerals just lying around on the side of the hill.) Anyway, Howard was singing, "Duke, Duke, Duke—Duke of Earl, Earl, Earl," in a deep voice, trying to sound funny, while I was still upset about that last fight between my parents, but I was also thinking how if Lily liked me, then I could forget about my home life, but if she never came around and noticed me, then I would be miserable forever.

Suddenly Howard dug a hunk of rock out of the dirt with his fingers and said, "Eureka!" Just enough of my brain was left over from thoughts about Lily and my family to be jealous of this fantastic rock that looked like petrified wood. Before I had time to get too jealous, though, he whacked the rock with another one so it broke in two, and handed half to me. "There you go, old chum," he said. And we both looked in awe at the insides of this rock, which were even more petrified wood–like than the outside, with parallel brown layers that might have been the tree's rings.

A guy who would share his treasure without thinking twice was a real friend—even if he did wear stupid bow ties to Assembly and always had dirty fingernails. So I decided to let him in on my secret.

"There's a girl I really like."

He shook his head in a blur, and said what dumbfounded people always say in cartoons: "Homina homina—huh?"

I told him who the girl was.

"Wow," he said respectfully. Then he asked if I had told her yet. I said grimly, "No."

"Are you going to?"

"I don't know."

That's when he dropped his bomb on me. "Well—what *are* you going to do about it?"

Until he asked the question, it never occurred to me that I *had* to do anything about it, except feel tormented. To cover up, I acted irritated. "If I knew *that,* I wouldn't be asking *you.*"

He said, "It's not that hard. Just ask her for a date."

Sure. Here he was, a guy with rocks bulging out of his pants pockets, who drew little 007s and James Bond guns on the cover of his loose-leaf, and he was telling me there was nothing hard about asking Lily for a date. There was no way in the world I could do it, since: a) people don't usually go on dates until they're about sixteen, and b) I had no idea what people did on dates, anyway.

"Where should you take her?" he wondered out loud. "How about the Hamburger Coach? That's where my brother takes girls. He says they love it when the little train comes around the track with the food."

"Hm," I said, while thinking, I can't take Lily there, that's where she had her birthday party in first grade and I spilled a milk shake on my shirt.

"Or the Empire State Building, that would be a great date. You could eat at the Automat first."

"My parents don't let me go into the city without them."

"Well, whatever you do, you'd better get cracking. If you don't ask her out, someone else will."

Just as my heart started to pound over that terrifying idea, which I must have been an idiot not to realize before, we spotted two guys from Nicky's old class coming up the hill, swinging white bulging socks that must have had ten pounds of chalk in them. We'd both forgotten that it was Halloween! Howard said, "Let's get out of here before they crack our skulls open," but I said, "No, over here," and we ducked behind the thickest, thorniest bushes on the hill, keeping quiet while the creeps yelled, "Come out, you fairies! You can't hide from us!"

Howard had a big grin as they walked right past us, but I wasn't smiling. I was squeezing my petrified wood and feeling sick with fear, because now I had to work up the nerve to ask Lily for a date.

chapter 3

Mr. Vigoritti said he wanted our class play, *Julius Caesar*, to be the finest production the school had ever seen. He told us what everyone knew as a rumor: that he was an amateur actor and opera singer himself. (That explained how his voice could reach to the other end of a noisy playground, and also why he decorated some of our bulletin boards with *Playbills* from *Oliver!* and *Camelot*.) He said that he had once sung in the chorus behind the opera star Robert Merrill, and that he hoped each of us would one day discover something we loved as much as he loved the theater.

When he asked for people to audition for the

role of Caesar, I did the most reckless thing of my life: I raised my hand. If I played the title role, I thought, then Lily might notice me in a different way and think of me as someone special. *Then* maybe I could invite her on a date.

I had it all planned . . . except that three other boys raised their hands, too, including Cary Lipshitz. Mr. Vigoritti told us to bring our chairs to the front of the room, and Cary's friends all cheered, "Go, C!" The four of us had to read the speech where Caesar says, "Cowards die many times before their deaths; the valiant never taste of death but once."

While waiting for my turn, I died about eight hundred deaths. It was dark gray outside, and pouring rain against the tall windows. Being brave long enough to raise your hand was one thing, but waiting and knowing you were about to make a fool of yourself in front of the whole class was a different story.

Raindrops dripped down the windows like sweat. I didn't notice that my hands were trembling until Cary made fun of me. "Chaikin's shakin'," he said under his breath. The people in the front row laughed.

"Settle down," Mr. Vigoritti called from the back, and pointed at me for my turn.

He had told us to think of Caesar as all-powerful
and contemptuous of lesser beings, so that's what
I tried to sound like. Unfortunately, it just came
out as loud.

Cary got the contemptuous part down pat,
but he sounded mean instead of powerful. And
the other guys didn't do so great, either. Mr.
Vigoritti folded his arms and thought it over.
Then he said, "I'd like to try something. Nicky,
would you please go to the front and read the
speech?"

Huh? What was going on? Did he want us to
hear a really *bad* performance, so we could do
the opposite?

He told Nicky, "Pretend you're the most
powerful man in the world—more powerful
than the president of the United States. You can
declare war, take slaves, sentence men to live or
die. You're Caesar—swaggering, superior, and
vain. Go ahead, give it a try."

Nicky hung his head down and read one sentence in the same mumble as always.

Mr. Vigoritti stopped him. "Nicky, I know
you're not shy. Come on, let 'er rip."

So he read the first sentence over again,
louder but still sounding about as excited as
somebody reading an instruction manual for a

35

vacuum cleaner. He obviously didn't want anything to do with the play.

No matter what he wanted, though, Mr. Vigoritti said, "I think I'm going to give Nicky his big break. Something tells me he's got what it takes to play Caesar, even if it's buried deep down."

Talk about humiliation—getting beat out by a guy who didn't even know the governor of New York was Rockefeller! As for Cary, forget it: the veins practically popped out of his forehead.

To make us feel better, Mr. Vigoritti asked me to audition for Brutus, and Cary for Antony. We both got the parts, but playing a traitor didn't seem like the best way to make Lily admire me. On the other hand, Mr. Vigoritti explained that Brutus was "the noblest Roman of them all," a man of conscience and ideals, so maybe it would work out in the end.

On the way back to our seats, Cary muttered to me, "Why doesn't he just get a chimpanzee to play Caesar?"

That turned out to be the last half-friendly thing he said to me for a long, long time.

Joseph Aptowitz lived in a big private house up on the hill, next door to Cary. He was the smartest kid in the class, the kind who got 100% on every test without studying, but he also acted crazy and immature and couldn't keep his shirt tucked in. On his birthday he invited most of the boys in the class to a party in his basement, with buckets of delicious Chicken Delight, which I had never tasted before, and a stack of 45s, including "Big Girls Don't Cry" and "Walk Like a Man." After some dignified debates about which cars people liked best and what caused the nuclear sub *Thresher* to sink, someone called out for Cary to do his J. F. K. impression. He jabbed with his finger, saying, "Ask not what your country can do for you . . . ," and then he did his Mr. Vigoritti, too, "Piggies at the trough!" Then he said, "Who's this?" and walked with his chin out in front and his eyes sleepy and his feet clomping on the floor like he wore size twelve shoes. We all knew immediately that it was Elliot, the tallest boy in the class and a friend of Cary's. Elliot was the only one who didn't laugh.

The next idea was to play a game they played at Cary's birthday party a few weeks before, where each person had to tell a secret about someone we all knew. You didn't have to be Albert Einstein to figure out that one of us was going to end up unhappy. What I didn't know was that it would be me.

Joseph told that Darlene Cohen had already had her first period (he knew because their big sisters were friends), and I told that Mrs. Weingold, the assistant principal, was really bald and her perky hair was a wig. People groaned, "Everyone knows that," but fortunately they didn't push me to come up with something else. Cary announced that Ronald Lindenbaum had a special exercise machine to help him lose some of his blubber, which cracked up the whole room but made me feel crummy at the same time, because his parents had taken me on their family trip to the Catskill Game Farm the summer before and treated me to crackers for the animals.

When it was Elliot's turn, he took a while to search his mind. I had never heard him say a mean word in his life, so I didn't expect any bombshells, but then he came out with this: "Cary likes Lily Wu."

The record playing at that moment was "Go Away Little Girl." "I know that your lips are sweet, but our lips must never meet." Suddenly the words felt like *my* story. If the coolest guy in the class wanted Lily, then our lips would never meet. Cary was smarter and more athletic than me, and even though he was basically nasty, people looked up to him because he was fearless.

"It's hurting me more each minute," the song said. Yeah, like getting hit in the face with a baseball bat.

Cary just rolled his eyes. He didn't deny that he liked Lily, he just said, "Big deal," and laughed— but the squeak at the end of the laugh gave him away.

I had a chicken drumstick in my hand, and put it down on my paper plate. While I rubbed the grease and crumbs off my fingers with some napkins, the next person took his turn and told a secret. It was Howard, saying, "Marc likes Lily, too. And he's going to ask her out."

Cary was right across from me. He didn't laugh in my face, he didn't destroy me with one of his sarcastic remarks. He just stared at me. I don't think he knew what to do any more than I did.

The other guys kidded around about how, personally, most of them preferred Debbie Winkler, who was wiggly and giggly and had a big smile full of teeth. Then Joseph got out his father's movie projector and showed some home movies of him and his kid brother clowning with toy swords and capes made out of white sheets. By the end of the party, he was running around the backyard with colored streamers flying from his nostrils, while people howled. Only two voices were missing from the laughter: two guys who had never done anything to each other but who had now become deadly enemies.

The Monday after the party, when I came down the ramp into the school yard after lunch, Cary called my name. He was near the handball courts, flipping baseball cards with a kid from another class. He asked if I had any cards on me. I always kept a few in my coat pocket to study statistics, but only the best ones, the players whose statistics you would care about, not the kind you gamble away. I didn't want to seem afraid of losing, though, so I said, "I've got some." He said, "Let's flip."

Cary had his own technique for flipping cards. He swung his arm back and forth in a relaxed way and then just let the card go twirling down to the ground. I had never believed that you could really control fronts or backs, but I found out I was wrong.

My first flip landed with the back up, unlike his. Good-bye, Whitey Ford.

As Cary bent to pick up the cards, he asked, "Are you still planning to ask Lily out?"

All I had to do was say, "Naw, she's just an old friend," and I would save myself a lot of pain. If I didn't give up, I knew he would find a thousand ways to embarrass me in front of Lily. And what chance did I have against him, anyway?

But I didn't want to give up. I didn't want to lose Lily, and also I had my pride. So I said, "Yeah, I am."

"Because you should know, this is serious for me. I *really* like her."

"So do I."

He let out a hoarse, nervous laugh, but didn't say anything else.

In the time it took to have our short conversation, he won not only my Whitey Ford, but also my Maury Wills, Tony Kubek, and Harmon Killebrew. He just put them in his pocket and walked away. That gave me a rough idea of what to expect from then on.

I once had a nightmare where a giant robot monster was roaming my neighborhood and looking for victims. I ducked behind a car, but he heard my sneakers drag on some pebbles, and then he stopped still, and his big metal head turned toward me. Even though I was behind the car, he was so big that he could see right over it, and if I didn't wake myself up, he would shoot disintegrating beams at me through his robot eyes.

What does that have to do with anything? This: in the past, Cary barely noticed I existed, but now he turned his death-ray eyes on me. Just like I had feared, he used every chance he got to make me look like an idiot. For example, once a week, each person had to report on some news story from the paper, like automation wiping out factory jobs, and then the class asked questions. Current events was my worst subject, because I never really understood the news. It all seemed so far away and unrelated to anything—like Martin Luther King Jr.'s March on Washington for civil rights; what did that have to do with us? Anyway, I reported on a Buddhist monk in Vietnam setting himself on fire as a protest (which *really* didn't make any sense to me), and Cary raised his hand and asked me to define "Buddhist." Not only couldn't I answer—I couldn't talk. Mr. Vigoritti tried to turn it around by assigning Cary to do a report on Buddhism the next week, but the embarrassment stayed stuck to me, not him.

Even worse, he started calling me "Spot" because of the mole above my lip. We had a Fall Field Day, and I won the sixty-yard dash, which should have been my moment of triumph, but he ruined it by making a wisecrack from the sidelines, "See Spot run." Howard said I should grab him and push his face into the pavement—but people in our class didn't do things like that, only the dumb kids did. And if I hit him, it would show that his insults had gotten to me. So I didn't say anything at all. Instead, I took my father's razor that afternoon and pulled it carefully over the mole, to scrape it away a little at a time. But I pressed too hard and cut myself, and had to put a little round Band-Aid on it to stop the bleeding. When I came out of the bathroom, my mother screamed because blood was dripping down around my mouth, and she dragged me back to the bathroom. "What happened to you?" she asked.

"I got hit by a baseball, it took a bad hop," I said.

She shook her head, not believing me, but when I peeked up there were tears in her eyes, over who knows what—maybe how bad things had gotten for both of us. We used to laugh and make jokes about all kinds of silly things, but now she was always whispering on the phone in her room with the door closed, and I had my own secret problems that were bad enough to make me cut up my face.

I was in the school bathroom when Cary came in and said, "Sorry to disappoint you, but Lily and I went on our first date over the weekend. We had a great time. We had ice-cream sodas at the White Fountain. I asked her to go steady, and she said yes. Tough luck, kiddo." He walked out and left me with blinding sunlight pouring through the pebbly window onto the side of my face. It was my own fault for waiting so long. What did I expect, when I gave him all the time in the world? I had known Lily for years, I'd had a million chances to talk to her, but never did—like in second grade, when she had been fourth in the girls' line and I had been fourth in the boys' line and we'd held hands every day. Now that would be the closest we ever came to being together.

After school, though, I saw Cary go talk to Lily outside, and she kind of shrunk up as he got closer, like he was the last person on Earth she wanted to see. It took me a while to figure out what was going on: that he had lied to me. They weren't going steady—I still had a chance!

He figured he could squash me like a bug, but

I kept popping back up, which infuriated him. Like when during a rehearsal of *Julius Caesar,* down on the auditorium stage, Brutus (played by me) was supposed to be calming down the crowd after we stabbed Caesar with our rubber daggers, and I ad-libbed by holding both hands up for silence. Cary said, "Chaikin surrenders," and everyone on the stage cracked up. But Mr. Vigoritti was sitting out in the seats and didn't hear that. He called out, "Bravo, Marc. *That's* what I meant about getting inside the scene. Excellent!" I could almost hear Cary's teeth grinding.

In spite of complimenting us now and then, Mr. Vigoritti got frustrated with our acting. One time he stopped the rehearsal and tried to make us understand the meaning of what we were saying. "This isn't a pageant," he said. "These events really happened. These men *lived.* And human nature hasn't changed since then. People still struggle for power. Small-minded men still murder great ones—it happened to Gandhi not that long ago. There are still idealists like Brutus and cynical manipulators like Cassius. Men still get caught up in conspiracies and mobs and do things they would never do alone. Just try to remember, when you say your lines, *a real person once lived this story.*"

That helped, and so did the time when he called us up to his desk to review our characters, one by one. He told me to never forget that Brutus was a noble person, even though he made a big mistake and let himself get sucked into the conspiracy to kill Caesar. He thought he was defending democracy against tyranny, but in the end his mistake destroyed him.

Because Mr. Vigoritti put so much work into coaching us, everyone improved—including Nicky, who turned into the best actor in the class. Instead of mumbling, he started playing Caesar like *Nicky,* the king of his old friends. When his wife begged him not to go to the Senate, he gave her a little shove to get past her, and Mr. Vigoritti applauded. That must have been the first time I saw Nicky smile, because I never knew until then that his teeth were crooked.

In the quiet after Mr. Vigoritti's applause, I heard someone talking under the stage by the piano. It was Lily, playing one of the mob, and she was so involved in what she was telling Julie that she didn't notice the quiet. Her face looked upset, not like herself. I couldn't even guess what would make her look like that.

Mr. Vigoritti scolded her. "Lily, please. We have to do this in front of the entire school in less than a month."

Although the auditorium was quiet before, it became dead-silent after. The whole class must have stopped breathing. Lily Wu getting yelled at? Everyone was in shock.

Everyone but me, that is. I had already noticed that something was bothering her lately. In the playground she always seemed to be talking to Julie with her face scrunched up. I couldn't remember the last time I had seen her smile her sweet old way. I wanted to hold her hands and look in her eyes and tell her that, no matter what the problem was, I would do anything to help. Except, how could I rescue her if I didn't have the nerve to talk to her?

I got my chance soon enough. On a day when rain leaked into the back of the classroom through the ceiling, Mr. Vigoritti sent Lily and me down to the office as monitors, to leave a note for the custodian. I had already figured out what to say to her: "Would you like to get some pizza with me after school? My treat." But once we were walking down the hall together, it didn't seem possible. How could I invite her for a date when I hadn't said two words to her since our Pizarro report? It would sound so out of the blue.

They had just mopped the floor, and it smelled like ammonia as we passed the color pictures of the astronauts along the wall. My guts were as tense as tennis racket strings. I just walked along with a dumb grin paralyzed on my face, imagining John Glenn and Alan Shepard yelling at me, "We risked our lives in space and you're too chicken to say, 'How's about getting some pizza together?'!"

You could hear our shoes on the floor and the electric clock buzzing high on the wall, that's how quiet it was. I kept peeking over at her in case she was peeking back at me, but she only stared at the floor ahead of us, like she was going over and over some upsetting problem in her head. I started to wonder if she would ever smile again.

But then she did. She said, "You're a fast runner," and gave me a small, friendly smile.

She still liked me! I was so excited, I couldn't figure out what she was talking about. Once I got it—that she meant the sixty-yard dash—I mumbled an answer: "When I have to, I just dig deep." But I couldn't find a next thing to say, so she went back to her secret thoughts, and I lost my best chance to mention pizza.

At the office, a tiny kindergartner was on the big oak bench, throwing up into a wastepaper basket. I had to fight to keep from getting sick myself. I put Mr. Vigoritti's note into the custodian's mailbox, and we headed back.

As we climbed back up the stairs, I asked myself, Why can't I talk to her? *Because I'm afraid,* was the obvious answer. That made me so mad at myself that I *forced* myself to talk. "You seem pretty quiet lately," I said.

She answered, "I guess I am."

"Is anything wrong?"

She giggled nervously, which didn't sound like her. "I'm just going crazy."

Mostly I wanted to giggle along with her and say, "Oh," making a joke of it, but I pushed myself to be brave. "Like how?" I asked.

She walked along, concentrating, maybe trying out words in her mind, maybe thinking she *could* talk to me about it. After all, I was probably her oldest friend. Telling me her problems might make her feel better.

But she couldn't do it. In the end she just said, "It's nothing. I don't know."

By then we were back in the Hall of the Astronauts again, walking past rooms 309 and 311 and 313, with that ammonia smell in our noses. I knew that now was my last chance to invite her out—but then we were at room 315, and 317, almost there. In my last few seconds, all I said was, "Phew, that ammonia stinks."

She replied, "It really does."

Then we were back in room 321, back in our seats, across the room from each other. That was that. Now Cary would ask her out, and I would lose her.

But at least that long walk was over.

Howard grabbed my arm after school and asked what happened. Did I pop the question? I told him the story, including that I was ready to give up. He said, "Are you nuts? She *likes* you. You can't give up before you even ask."

He made me vow to ask her out the next day, no matter what. I agreed, thinking a vow would force me to go through with it.

The problem was, I never saw her alone the next day. We had a class trip to the *Long Island Press,* to see how a newspaper gets published, and didn't get back to school till almost two. But I refused to break my vow, so at three o'clock I ran up to her and Julie as they were walking home. "Hi," I said, like we were three old friends who always walked home together.

Julie said, "Howdy," trying not to seem surprised, but Lily looked a bit annoyed, as if I had interrupted a private conversation.

Julie walked between us. Or, actually, I purposefully ran up next to Julie instead of Lily, so I wouldn't seem too obvious. I had a plan, though. As soon as Julie turned off into the court where she lived, that's when I would ask Lily to go with me to Lorenzo's for pizza.

Julie said to me, "So, do you know your rods from your cones?" because we had just learned how the eye works in the last hour of school.

That gave me my cue of how I could talk to them. Instead of acting all serious and mature, I joked back. "Strange things are happening in Mr. Vigoritti's classroom. When he turns the lights out, his pupils get bigger."

Julie groaned and said, "You have an extremely vitreous humor." I came back with, "I've never heard a cornea joke than that," and she replied, "Ha! You've got a lot of optic nerve."

Lily was smiling! I was amazed at how great I was doing—that is, until Cary came up next to her at the corner and said, "Can anyone join this party?"

Since Lily didn't answer, Julie said, "Eye-eye, sir."

I was too frustrated to laugh. The four of us crossed the street together, looking like a double date with me next to the wrong girl. Cary turned the subject around to how Mr. Vigoritti had blown his top in the bus coming back from the newspaper (because Joseph kept making people laugh with his plastic vampire fangs, which annoyed the editor who gave us the tour). Cary said one day Mr. Vigoritti's head would pop open and molten lava would come shooting out. Julie laughed—but not Lily, because she was looking down the street, down the hill, at some other kids walking home. So at least she wasn't in love with Cary (yet).

"Lily," he said next, and my heart stopped, afraid he would ask her out right then and there, just to humiliate me. "You've got to stop getting 100's on everything. You're making the rest of us look bad."

She tried to smile, but it came out tense. He kept going anyway. "You're studying too much! Unless you're just a genius like Joseph."

Lily kept quiet, so Julie teased her too. "All

she ever does is work. I bet if she didn't study, she'd be as dumb as everyone else."

"Never!" I shot in, trying to keep up with Cary in case his flattery was getting through to her. "She's too smart."

"There are lots of smart people in the class," Cary said. "But only one who's beautiful, too."

"And sweet," I said, and my face turned red, because that was practically like announcing to the world how I felt.

Lily looked down at the ground, hiding from our compliments. "I think you've got some ad*mi*-rers," Julie sang.

Lily gave her a stunned look. Believe it or not, until then I don't think she got it, that Cary and I both liked her. Frankly, I wanted to kick Julie in the behind.

We had reached the court where Julie lived. *"Adios, amigos,"* she said. "Everybody behave yourselves."

And she left us to finish the duel without her.

We kept walking. It was a windy day, and bits of dusty dirt from the bald patches in the grass rose up and swirled around us. I couldn't think of a single thing to say.

It took Cary to get us started again. "My father is talking about buying a Piper Comanche," he said. "That's what I want to do—learn to fly, circle around the Empire State Building and the Statue of Liberty. We went up in a small plane this summer, upstate. It's the coolest thing. Did you ever fly, Lily?"

She whispered, "No."

"Maybe we can take you up for a ride."

She didn't answer. To stay in the competition, I made up an ambition. "I'm thinking about joining the Peace Corps after college. Go to Africa, help people in the jungle. Did you ever think about doing that, Lily?"

"No," she mumbled.

The wind blew her hair around into her face, and she didn't push it away, she hid behind it. Cary said to me, "You can't get into the Peace Corps unless you have a skill. What's your skill—flipping baseball cards?"

I said, "No, brain surgery. Maybe I can cure *you*."

"Better work on yourself first," he said, and touched his own lip on the place where I have my mole.

Now I *really* wanted to kill him—but I couldn't start a fight in front of Lily, so I just said, "Why don't you shut up?"

We were behind Lily's apartment, by the

rusted old clotheslines that didn't have any wire between the poles. Lily looked about as happy as Joan of Arc getting burned at the stake.

Cary ignored me and started talking to Lily about things I knew nothing about, like horseback riding and sailboats. I just tagged along and felt hopeless. He lived in the exact opposite direction, but he came a mile out of his way just so I wouldn't get her to myself.

The three of us ended up on her stoop together. He said to me, "I think I hear your mother calling," and I snapped back, "No, you're just having those hallucinations again." Then the wind blew hard, and Lily got something in her eye. With one hand rubbing the tears, she whispered, "I have to go," and disappeared inside the front door.

We heard her feet hurrying up the stairs. I wanted to tell Cary off, that he was wrong to assume he was better than everyone else, because he was really just a jerk—but he didn't wait to hear it, he turned his back and left with a disgusted *Tsk,* like he couldn't stand to be within ten feet of me.

While walking home across the ball field, and then while I ate my apple in the kitchen and Mom did the dishes, I tried to figure out what Lily might be thinking. Neither one of us had made a very good impression, that much I knew. And she definitely didn't seem thrilled to find out we both liked her. But that might have been because of shyness—all that attention hurt her, like a too-bright light shining in her eyes. Maybe she *did* like one of us but was upset because now she would have to hurt the other one's feelings. She had probably never hurt anyone in her whole life.

My mother shut the water off and turned around to face me. "We haven't been talking much lately," she said.

I shrugged.

"You're having a hard time, aren't you?"

I was too embarrassed to give her any details, and I didn't want her pinching my cheek and saying, "My little boy's in love!" So I just said, "It's nothing."

"You used to let me make it better when something hurt," she said sadly.

The funny thing is, I *wanted* to tell somebody. But I couldn't. I just chewed on a piece of apple and didn't say anything.

She said, "Let me tell you something. What's going on between your father and me, it's not your fault. You didn't cause our problems, so don't blame yourself. Okay?"

The whole time, we were talking about two different things: me about Lily, and her about their fights. She had no idea what was going on!

"Marc?"

"All right, all right, I won't blame myself."

"You don't have to get mad at me." She turned toward the sink so I wouldn't see her cry.

Now I had one more thing to feel lousy about.

chapter 4

Allen Deutsch, the class artist, led a committee to make the sets for *Julius Caesar* in his apartment. I helped out once, by cutting around the outlines of the Roman columns he painted.

We never got to see the sets finished, though, because when Allen brought the rolled-up paintings to school, three guys from Nicky's old class beat him up and tore the paper to shreds. They said they would bash his head in with a brick if he told who did it, so he chucked the pieces in a Dumpster and lied to Mr. Vigoritti that his baby sister had ripped the scenery apart.

The attacks were heating up, and so was the anger in our class. So far, we had only taken small kinds of revenge. When Joseph Aptowitz got beat up in the abandoned playground by Fat Ralph Sawicki and another kid, some guys from our class yelled out in the school yard, "Fat Ralph has fat lips, Fat Ralph has fat lips." He socked one of them in the belly, but a teacher saw him and pulled him against the fence. Then, on Halloween, Charles Grinsberg got bombarded with eggs by Fat Ralph and Matty Parisi, a short kid who was always combing his hair. Charles had big buck teeth, and Cary's friends teased him about it all the time—he was pathetic enough without having yellow eggs dripping down his jacket while he ran home crying. Scott Siegel saw it happen and told everyone about it, and the next day, Ralph and Matty got mustard squirted on their backs while our two classes were crossing in the stairwell.

The whole feud seemed stupid to me. I had more serious business to think about, like what I should do about Lily. Fighting with jerks was the last thing on my mind—but I got dragged in against my will.

What happened was, Elliot spotted Mickey Mantle going into Lorenzo's Pizza, and he called Joseph, who called Howard, who called me, saying we should run over there for autographs, *fast*.

I grabbed the cleanest one of my three baseballs, which was a lighter brown than the other two, and washed it with soap under the bathroom faucet (it didn't help), then sprinted all the way to the pizzeria.

There were four guys from our class in front of Lorenzo's when I got there, and four from 6-309, all arguing about who would go in first. It was the dumbest thing I ever saw. "What are we standing out here for?" I shouted, still out of breath. "Let's all just go in,"—but a pimply kid named Ray Casey blocked the door and said, "You're not going nowhere."

He had to move, though, because Mickey Mantle came out right then in a sports jacket and tie, drinking soda from a paper cup. "Excuse me," he said. He had a kid with him, also wearing a jacket and tie, who looked like maybe a fifth grader. You could see the resemblance between their faces.

Every part of him was bigger than any man we had ever seen: his neck, his hands, his thighs. He was like a redwood tree. He put his hand on his boy's shoulder and was going to walk past us, but Joseph said, "Mr. Mantle, could we have your autograph?"

He didn't smile. He looked like, *I can't even stop for a slice of pizza without a bunch of brats pester-*

ing me. But the boy said, "Go ahead, Dad," and so he asked, "Who's got a pen?"

About seven of us did. He signed his name on everyone's piece of paper and on my baseball. It was like meeting J. F. K. or the astronauts—I couldn't make myself look into his eyes. Even when he said to me, "This ball's wet," I was too embarrassed to explain why, and he didn't bother asking questions.

One guy asked him how his injured foot felt, and he said, "Better, thanks." That was it for conversation. On my way over there, I had imagined how great it would be if he spent a few minutes talking to us and said some words of wisdom that I would remember for the rest of my life, but he obviously just wanted to get out of there. I wouldn't like it either if nine strangers surrounded me and my son. Anyway, without looking back, he unlocked a white Cadillac that was about twice as long as my family's Rambler, and they drove away.

While we were watching his tail fins, something yanked at my hand. It was Matty, trying to grab my baseball. I yelled, "Get your hand off that ball!" Howard pulled him away, and then Fat Ralph shoved Howard and came after the ball, saying, "Give it." I ended up running, because I didn't want to risk losing the ball in a fight, and Howard went with me. Ralph clucked after us, "Buk buk buk buk," like a chicken, but Howard yelled back, "Maybe you could catch us if you weren't so fat and stupid." So then Ralph and Matty chased us for two blocks (thanks a lot, Howard), but we're both fast so we got away.

From then on, I hated 6-309's guts—the whole class. Because of them, I had to flee down the street like a coward two minutes after meeting Mickey Mantle. That must be how feuds work: no matter how wise you think you are, once some bully turns you into a victim, your anger gets the upper hand over your brains.

A couple days later, Ralph and pimply Ray waited for Howard on his way back to school after lunch. He was carrying his giant poster on air pollution, which he had worked on every day for two weeks. They ambushed him by the same abandoned playground where they got Joseph, the one where the seesaws had broken handles and there were no swings at the bottoms of the chains. He ended up with a ripped sleeve on his coat, a crushed poster, a cut on his cheek, and bits of white concrete grit all over. Howard is even skinnier than me, so this went past bullying into something like a crime.

I was already in the school yard when Howard got there. Seeing his cuts, I put my arm around his shoulder and led him fast around the handball courts, over to the yellow home plate of the punchball diamond. One by one, the guys from our class noticed the blood on his face and came over.

He was breathing hard from anger, and he wanted revenge. Seeing his blood, I was ready to go over and fight those creeps right then and there. I was so mad, I thought I could beat them just by the power of my fury. Even if I got hurt, I would at least get some punches in. We could see the two of them by the basketball court, glancing our way like they were scared a whole mob of us would come after them. "Let's go," I said.

"Hold on," Elliot said, "let's take care of Howard first," and he went over to wet his handkerchief at the water fountain so we could clean off Howard's face. On the way back, he brought Cary.

"I want to kill those pigs," Howard said while Elliot wiped his face. "I want to bash their skulls together."

He was always fantasizing himself as some kind of superhero, or James Bond, knocking bad guys around like punching bags. The difference between his fantasies and his skinny, messed up self was so gigantic, it made you embarrassed for him.

Cary didn't take this too seriously. To him, Howard was a nobody. He just said, "Their brains are only matched by their good looks."

Other people were angrier, though, especially the ones who had already been beaten up. "They're garbage," Charles squeaked. "They're worthless!"

"Look at them, they must be three times his size."

"They should go to reform school for this!"

Most of our class wanted to fight, but they had to work themselves up more in order to do it since it might mean getting suspended from school, and since it also might get bloody.

Meanwhile, on the basketball court, the guys from 6-309 were joining up with Ralph and Ray. They saw us talking together and they knew what was up. We had waited too long—if we attacked now, it would turn into a giant battle instead of quick revenge.

But Howard didn't care about that. He said, "Come on," and started walking. We couldn't let him down, so three or four of us followed him, and then the rest came along so they wouldn't look bad.

"Look at those faces," he said. "They're like something from *The Twilight Zone*."

It was true. They had nasty mouths and squinty eyes—and they didn't get any handsomer up close.

Howard said to Ralph and Ray, "You think you're so tough. Wait till we get *you* alone."

Ralph said, "Uh-oh, I better start carrying my flyswatter."

Joseph said, "If you ever took a bath, you wouldn't *need* a flyswatter."

Ralph said, "Okay, Mouth, you want your teeth busted, you got it."

I said, "Yeah, how many guys are you gonna bring with you? Ten?"

Little Matty said, "That's all they got is lip. They can't fight for nothing."

"You think any of you could win a fight against me?" Ralph said. "I'll meet you after school any day."

His arms alone must have weighed twice as much as me, but I said, "How about today?"

"Hold on," Howard said. "*I'm* the one who should fight him."

It went on like that, with nobody actually taking a swing but both sides threatening and insulting each other more and more (because if you didn't answer every insult with a worse one, then you were the loser) until Matty said, "There's Nicky, I'm gonna go get him."

Nicky was off by himself studying his *Julius Caesar* script by the fence. He came over and stood between the two mobs, looking annoyed about the interruption. "What's the problem?" he said.

Matty told him how Ralph and Ray had beat up this loser, and now his whole class was making a stink. Nicky asked Ralph why they did it, and Ralph said, "He insulted me."

Howard said, "I did not!"

"Lying little runt," Ralph said.

Before it went any further, I reminded Howard about when we ran away with my autographed baseball.

"What did you say?" Nicky asked Howard.

Suddenly he remembered the "fat and stupid" comment and repeated it to Nicky, who said, "What do you expect when you say something like that?"

Howard got indignant. "Yeah, an insult is the same as ripping someone's coat and pushing his face into the sidewalk. That's only fair. That's great logic."

Nicky gave him a stare like a warning. "If you said that to me, I'd tear your throat out."

Howard said, "They were trying to steal his baseball with Mickey Mantle's autograph!"

Some of the other class started laughing in an exaggerated way, like what Howard said was ridiculous. Cary said, "I believe I hear hyenas."

Ray said, "Watch your mouth," and Cary said, "It speaks!"

That got to Nicky. "This is my class you're talking to. You say something about them, you're saying it about me."

Cary rolled his eyes.

Nicky said, "Somebody's got to teach you about respect," and jabbed his finger into Cary's shoulder.

In all of elementary school, I had only seen Cary get mad a couple times, and this was one of them. He stared Nicky down and said, "No, I know all about respect. It means respecting people who *deserve* it."

In Nicky's face you could see him pounding Cary into chopped meat. But the outside Nicky didn't move. I remembered what he had told Cary on the bus at the Morris-Jumel Mansion: one more fight and Mr. Eisenman would expel him.

Ralph and Ray came up and grabbed Cary's arms. "We got him, Nicky," Ray said.

Cary yanked himself free with a look of cold rage. And that's when Mr. Vigoritti showed up. "What's going on here?" he asked us.

We all looked down.

"All right, *I'll* tell *you*," he said. "The same idiocy as last year and the year before that. It baffles me how intelligent boys can let themselves get drawn into this brutish nonsense. Every year I hope my students will behave more sensibly than the world's leaders, and every year I see the same mindless violence. It's a good thing you don't have bombs to drop on each other."

He looked hard at Joseph and me and a few others. "*Please* don't act like this. You know better. I hope at least some of you can hear what I'm saying."

I heard him, and what he said made sense, but he didn't understand that we had to defend our pride. Just like our fathers had gone to World War II and risked their lives to beat the Nazis—they were *heroes,* even if it was hard to imagine it now that they were middle-aged— we had to stand up for ourselves against these animals who thought they could trample us for fun. It wasn't acting like a mob; it was a matter of honor.

Mr. Vigoritti went back to his group of teachers,

but he kept his eye on us. Howard was still worked up, though. He said, "I don't care if we get caught. I'm ready."

"Watch out," Matty said. "He might throw a punch and faint from the strain."

"Or bweak his wittle hand."

Mr. Vigoritti's talk had given me time to cool off a bit, but their insults got me going again. Words rushed out of me before I knew what I was saying. "Okay, why talk anymore? Let's settle it, once and for all. Your whole class against our whole class—off school property, so no one can stop us. We'll see how tough you are when it's not three against one."

Nicky said, "That's not a fight, that's a war."

But his old classmates liked the idea. "Yeah," Ralph said, "us against the pip-squeaks."

Cary said, "This is idiotic," but Allen, whose paintings they had ripped up, said, "No it's not."

"Who says we do it?" Howard asked, and raised his hand.

I put my hand up, and then so did everyone else. Finally we were going to join together and fight back! It felt like patriotism.

Only Nicky and Cary didn't raise their hands. Matty said, "Come on, Nicky, you're with us, right?"

He didn't mention getting expelled, he just shook his head in disgust. "It makes no sense."

Right then a little girl, a fourth grader, probably, bumped into him while chasing one of those big red mushy balls. She caught him off balance, and he fell over.

Everyone shut up. His script with his speeches underlined had landed open on the ground next to him. Nicky automatically grabbed the girl by the arm, but then he saw how small she was and shoved her away. He looked at his friends, who watched him in a confused way, like, was he trying to duck out of this fight? Then he said, "Okay. If you all want to make fools of yourselves—when do we do it?"

Howard said, "Three o'clock. Right after school." But Elliot and some of the others had a Scout meeting. Howard wanted to do it the next school day, which was Monday—but if we all showed up on Tuesday with scabs and black eyes, our teachers would figure out what happened and we would get in big trouble. So we agreed to meet the next Friday, one week later, under the trees on top of Suicide Hill, where no one could see us. That way we would have the weekend for any wounds to heal.

Howard and Nicky made up the rules for the

fight. No sticks or rocks or other weapons. An even number on both sides. Once you got beat, you had to go home. After a half hour of fighting, we would count who had the most guys left, and that class would be the undisputed winner. Ralph and Ray wanted the winning class to kick the whole losing class in the backsides, but everyone else said no because it sounded so stupid.

While we made these plans, Cary stood there shaking his head, like he was watching a bunch of monkeys reenact the Battle of Gettysburg—an amazing and ridiculous spectacle. But when Elliot asked him, "You're coming, right?" he said, "Looks like I don't have any choice."

By then, nobody seemed all that furious anymore. But we had a whole week to remind ourselves of everything those morons had done to us, and get enraged again.

A teacher at the top of the ramp put up the two fingers for quiet. All over, kids' arms shot up obediently with their fingers in Vs as they went silent. Our corner got quiet, too. Recess was over, and the whole playground had turned just as peaceful and orderly as the principal wanted it—except that, behind our good behavior, we were imagining a bloody slaughter.

chapter 5

By that night I already wished I hadn't opened my big mouth in the playground. Nicky was right, starting World War III made no sense at all—especially if there was no way your side could win. And Mr. Vigoritti was right about all this fighting being just plain wrong. But we couldn't back out now or we would be disgraced.

Brutus let himself get involved in a murder plot that ended up being his downfall. Unlike him, I could see my mistake beforehand—but I couldn't see any way out.

That Sunday my father sat slumped on the couch watching a Giants game while Mom read one of her big fat paperback biographies in their bedroom. I wandered into the living room for no particular reason, and he patted the couch next to him. "Come watch the game with me," he said. So I sat down, and he reached over and squeezed my knee. "How's my buddy?" he asked. I guess he was unhappy about their battles, too, and wanted to see at least one friendly face around the house.

We had never had a heart-to-heart talk, but I was desperate for help. The more I thought about how we had gotten sucked into fighting those jerks, when no one in our class knew how to fist fight, the more I wanted to ask him for advice.

We watched Frank Gifford make a great diving catch, and then a ref made a bad call and my father pointed at the screen and said, "Watch, he's going to throw his helmet." He was right—Y.A. Tittle threw his helmet down on the ground, which he only did when he was furious, and on the next play there was a big, angry clash at the scrimmage line, but the halfback broke free and scored a touchdown.

In all that time, I never said a word. Starting an important conversation with my father wasn't much easier than asking Lily for a date. The truth is, he didn't like to hear about problems. He hated when anything bad happened to anyone in the family, and he got so upset that when things went wrong, no one even wanted to tell him.

Then, a cigarette commercial came on, "Tareyton smokers would rather fight than switch." Seeing the guy with the black eye finally gave me a way to begin. "Did you ever get a black eye?" I asked my father.

He said, "No. Why?"

"Did you ever get in any big fights?"

He turned to look at me and asked again, suspiciously, "Why?"

"I was just curious." I tried to sound very casual, like he had no reason to worry. "Did a bunch of your friends ever fight a bunch of other guys?"

Now he gave me his Red Hot Iron Spear look. "You're not in a gang, are you?" he asked.

"No," I said, glad to get out of it without lying.

"Because that would be the worst mistake you ever made. *Never* join a gang."

"I'm not joining a gang."

"I don't care if all your friends are doing it, *don't*. Gangs have no purpose except to fight. They start with fists and the next thing you know, it's knives. I don't want to hear about you going to the hospital because of a gang fight. Understand?"

"I'm not in any gang!"

But he kept hammering at his point. "Listen to me, this is important. I can't be with you every second to protect you. I wish I could, but I can't. You're going to have to learn some judgment. Just stay away from fights. I know you, you're not the violent type. I'd rather have you run away from a fight than let some kid twice your size hurt you. Do you hear me?"

"Yes, yes, yes!"

And I went to my room and slammed the door, just like my mother always did, because you couldn't talk to him, he never helped, he only twisted things around and didn't listen and left you more upset than you were before.

Since I couldn't see any way out of the battle, I tried not to think about it. Instead, I sat on the couch and pulled back the curtain to look over at Lily's apartment across the ball field. The leaves had fallen off the trees by then, so I could see the window of her room up on the second floor, but she was never in it.

One time I saw a guy walk up to her front

door in a blue ski jacket with red zigzags—Cary's jacket! He didn't go in at first, he just stood there on the stoop, like he had to get up his nerve. *Go home,* I commanded him by mental telepathy, just in case it might work.

Then he knocked, the door opened, and he went inside.

So much for my mental powers.

I had to decide what to do, and fast. If he convinced her to go out with him, they might end up going steady for real. (But how could she say yes to such a conceited jerk? It wouldn't be fair!) I might never get my chance with her, all because I didn't take action RIGHT NOW.

The brave thing to do would have been to rush over there and make sure he didn't get in ahead of me. And, surprise—that was exactly what I did. I ran out without even a coat, watching my breath make clouds, and planned the Final Showdown. This had gone on long enough. It was time for her to pick one of us, once and for all. To be honest, I was so sick of the torment that hearing, "I'm sorry, Marc," would have been a relief compared to things going on and on the same way.

I knocked and heard footsteps coming down the stairs—adult-size footsteps.

Lily's mother said from behind the door, "Who's there?"

"It's Marc Chaikin." Since she hadn't seen me in years and probably didn't remember me, I added, "A friend of Lily's."

When the door opened, she gave me a big smile, which helped. "Hello, Marc! We haven't seen you in so long. You've grown so tall!"

Lily had the prettiest mother of my friends. She wasn't fat like mine or Howard's, and she always wore a nice dress, even at home in the middle of the day. She led me upstairs into their living room, which they had decorated in a fancier way since my last visit. There were a lot of new things to see, including a blue parakeet in a cage, a tropical fish tank with a glowing light inside, two Chinese vases with scenery painted on them, a shiny black piano against one wall . . . and Lily and Cary sitting on the couch, separated only by about three feet.

Cary had on a string tie. That made him seem more respectful than me, whose nose was running from the cold. He gave me a look like a tomahawk thrown at my face. Lily just stared down at her lap. I felt bad for putting her in this awkward situation. (Or, actually, I feel bad *now*, but at the time I was too nervous to think much about her point of view.)

"Oh—hi," I said, acting surprised to find Cary there. "I just thought I would come say hello."

Mrs. Wu told me to have a seat, so I sat on a chair with turquoise cushions. She stood in the kitchen doorway, waiting to enjoy our conversation. When nobody talked, she said, "Lily, you haven't offered your friends anything to drink."

Hardly looking up, Lily asked us, "Would you like soda or milk or orange juice?"

Her mother said, "Or I could make hot chocolate."

Cary said, "Nothing for me, thank you."

"I just had something at home," I lied. "Thanks, anyway."

Coming right out and asking Lily who she liked better, me or Cary, didn't seem so simple anymore, with her mother smiling at us encouragingly from the doorway.

Where to put my eyes became a problem. There were photos of Lily and her brothers on top of the piano, so I looked at those. In one picture her oldest brother was standing in front of some old-fashioned stone buildings. Mrs. Wu saw me looking and said, "Thomas is a pre-med student at Yale. Henry is applying to college now. He wants to go to M.I.T."

I said, "Wow. You must be proud of them."

She said, "Of course! But Lily will make us proud, too. We're planning for her to go to Juilliard."

I had no idea what Juilliard was; I thought she was saying, "Julie Yard." Was that like Scotland Yard? Luckily I didn't ask, because two seconds later, Cary said to Lily, "I didn't know you played an instrument."

Mrs. Wu laughed. "You didn't know Lily won a state competition last year? She performed at Carnegie Hall, in a recital! Play something for your friends, Lily. Play the Chopin you've been practicing."

"I'm just learning it," Lily said, and didn't move.

Her mother said, "Lily . . ." still smiling, but in a way that her daughter couldn't disobey.

So, over to the piano she went, with a dead face that made me sorry I had pushed my way in. Suddenly I knew what she had meant when she said, "I'm going crazy," that day in the halls. It was just like long ago, in kindergarten, when I was over here playing with her: Lily's brother Thomas wanted to go out and play ball with his friends, but Mrs. Wu said, "Your science project is due in two weeks!" and made him stay in his room to work on it. Even though she was nice to me, I could see she wouldn't let her children be anything but perfect—and Lily wasn't the type to yell or say, "I refuse."

She lifted the cover off the piano keys and played some very quick, skipping classical music, without smiling once. If there was a difference between her and a professional musician, I couldn't hear it. She reminded me of a TV surgeon, not noticing anything but the task in front of her. Her fingers moved so fast, you couldn't even see them clearly.

Suddenly, though, she stopped playing and said, "I have to practice this one more." I guess she had hit a wrong note, but I couldn't hear it.

Her mother gave a disappointed sigh and said, "Why don't you take your friends to your room and play a game, then, while I cook dinner?"

Lily kept staring at the piano keys and didn't answer.

"You can play Scrabble."

Lily still didn't move. Without looking up, she murmured, "I have to do my homework," but her mother said, "You're so serious, Lily! You have two nice friends visiting. You can do your homework after dinner."

So we finally made it to Lily's room, in private—the exact thing I had planned on, except that she was walking ahead of us like a prisoner of war going to the torture chamber.

Her room was extremely neat—no dust anywhere, the curtains in perfect S-ripples. She was the only person I knew who had her own set of World Book Encyclopedias, but she didn't have anything personal around, just a picture of flying ducks on the wall that I remembered from when we were little. Between school and the piano, she probably worked too hard to have time for hobbies like rock-hunting or building models.

She climbed onto a chair and got her Scrabble set down from the closet. Then she sat on the floor, unfolded the board, and started turning over tiles one at a time in the box, so the letters didn't show.

Watching her fingers turn over the tiles, I got hypnotized. I wanted to say, "Stop, Lily, we have to talk," but instead I fell into a trance, just watching.

Cary sat down on the wood floor next to her and helped. I snapped out of it and sat on the other side of her so I could help too.

"Go ahead and pick letters," she said.

Cary got a B, so he went first. He put down the word SPHERE, and gave me a glare, like, *Now you'll learn not to butt in.* He was so determined to crush me, he didn't notice how unhappy Lily was.

She made a nothing word, TIP, and then it was my turn. Concentrating, I came up with something clever: I made TOOTH down (using the H in SPHERE) and TO and IT across. But that still gave me only half as many points as him.

Next he said, "Okay, Spot," and got two double letter scores and a double word score with SERV-ICE.

Instead of insulting him back, I said coolly, "Winner take all."

I'm pretty sure he knew what I meant (though hopefully Lily didn't). Whoever lost would go home and let the other one ask Lily out.

When he didn't answer, I said, "Scared?"

He said, "Of you?" and snickered. "It's your funeral."

So, like Godzilla versus King Kong, both of us put down colossal words and then the other one came back with an even more stupendous one. He got two triple word scores, but I got a fifty-point bonus for using all seven letters with the word QUESTING. Actually, Lily jumped into first place for a while (she got a triple word score with VIZIER, which I'd never heard of before), and that confused the issue, but she didn't really have her mind on the game, and we left her behind a few turns later.

In spite of giving it everything I had, I couldn't stay ahead. We kept playing leapfrog, back and forth. At first nobody talked much—except when Cary challenged my ZEAL and we found it in Lily's paperback dictionary, ha! There was just the click of the wooden tiles and Walter Cronkite reporting the news out in the living room, with the sound of Mrs. Wu chopping vegetables almost drowning him out. But then Cary started talking to Lily during my turns, about how *she* should have gotten picked instead of Darlene Cohen to represent us at the Public School United Nations, because she was smarter, nicer, and prettier, too. It was hard to think about words with all that chattering. Not that it got him anywhere—she looked sick to her stomach, not flattered—but he did manage to throw off my concentration.

Since he did it to me, I did it to him, too. While he searched the crowded board for possible spaces, I asked Lily how long she had played the piano. She mumbled, "Since I was five." I said enthusiastically, "Wow, that's young," but she didn't seem very impressed with herself. "Some people start at three," she said softly.

It became harder and harder to find room for our words, even with good letters. The parakeet in the other room started running back and forth on its little swing and chirping like it had suddenly gone berserk from being cooped up, and that made it even harder to think. I had to put down puny three-letter words more than once. After I put down PAT, Cary sneered, "Very impressive," which almost forced me to choke him. But the good guys came out victorious in the end: a double word score on QUIZ put me way ahead.

Cary exploded. "You son of a bitch!" he growled. "You took my space!"

"Grow up," I said.

"You keep getting in my way and you'll regret it."

His face had turned dark. Although I was worried that he would fly at me over the Scrabble board, I said, "Big threats."

"You want to go downstairs and see if I mean it?"

A noise came from Lily, like the beginning of a groan she couldn't keep inside any longer.

I said to Cary, "Just shut up, she doesn't want to hear this." Then I asked Lily, "Are you okay?"

She stood up and went over near the door.

Above her head was that painting of ducks flying toward the sun.

Cary apologized. "I'm sorry, Lily, I lost my temper."

She looked down at the floor and said, "You both have to leave."

I wish I could take back what I said next. I just wanted to get this rivalry settled—so, without thinking about how Lily felt, I said, "Can't we just finish the game?"

She never looked up, she just stayed there under the ducks. "You have to go away, both of you," she said. "I know you like me, but I'm sorry, I don't feel that way about you. I just want you both to leave me alone."

Neither Cary nor I stood up to go, so Lily explained more. "I never wanted to disappoint anyone. I know how much it hurts to like someone when they don't feel the same way. Because there's someone *I* like, and he'll never notice me."

So, first the girl of my dreams stuck a sword through my chest, and then she twisted it around. Cary sat behind his rack of Scrabble letters like a pile of bones, not even watching her.

Although I could hardly stand to know the answer, I got up my courage and asked, "Is it someone in our class?"

"Yes."

"Who?" I asked, thinking, Elliot? Joseph? and hoping to God it wasn't Howard.

She shook her head like she didn't want to tell. But then she whispered, "Nicky."

Cary jerked, like someone had shot ten thousand volts through his almost-dead body. He said, "WHAT?!"

She kept her voice down so her mother wouldn't hear. "People are wrong about him. He's not that bad. And I hate the way you—" (uh-oh!) "—make fun of him." (Whew, she was talking to Cary.) "I don't care if he doesn't get good marks. He does whatever he wants, he's not afraid of anything."

So, instead of liking me, or even Cary, she preferred a guy who beat people up, who came to school in shirts without a collar and got sent home, who never knew a right answer in all the times he got called on. It made as much sense as a sparrow falling in love with a shark. No matter what, it couldn't work out.

All of my guts wanted to say, "But he's so *dumb.*" There wasn't any use pointing that out, though. If she liked him, it didn't matter, because she would never like me.

"I'm sorry," she said. "I know how you feel.

Because he acts like I'm nothing, just a boring nobody."

I expected her to order us to leave again, but instead she said, "You think I'm crazy, don't you?"

I couldn't argue. I just shrugged.

Standing up, I tapped Cary on the shoulder and said, "Let's go." He got up and followed me out.

Mrs. Wu was chopping green peppers with a meat cleaver and throwing them into a giant metal pot shaped like a bowl. She stirred the peppers with a chopstick and they sizzled. "Who won the game?" she asked cheerfully.

I said, "Nobody."

Outside, it had gotten dark and cold, but Cary didn't put on his ski jacket, and I didn't have a coat. Neither of us walked away at first. We just stood on the stoop like two animals that had gotten shot in the head but hadn't fallen down yet.

A noisy bus went by, a roar in the middle of the quiet. Inside, people were reading papers or dozing or looking out the window. For them, this was an ordinary night. They had no idea what had just happened to us. If they saw us at all, they probably thought we were two ordinary boys without a care in the world.

I kept thinking, *Nicky?!* But I was too upset to say it out loud.

Cary didn't talk either. For once in his life, he had no wisecrack to make, no put-downs, no way to pretend the situation was beneath him. In the end he just walked away into the dark.

That day knocked something out of him. I didn't hear him say another sarcastic word the rest of the year.

chapter 6

While sitting on the couch the next afternoon and staring at the same homework question for an hour ("Why were Guy and Matthew trapping muskrats?"), I heard my mother on the phone in her bedroom. I couldn't tell if she was laughing or crying. I heard her say something about how it was all settled, from tonight on, it didn't concern her anymore. If he wanted a girlfriend, fine, now he could see her whenever he wanted.

So my father had a girlfriend—and that meant I didn't have a family anymore. I had to fight to hold the swollen feeling inside, because it felt like my chest was going to bust apart. Now I understood what all the fighting and yelling was really about. By tonight, he would be gone.

No one I knew had divorced parents. And I'd never *heard* of a father having a girlfriend before. The whole situation seemed weird and horrible. No one else's family had such awful things going on in it. Only mine.

He came home earlier than usual from his night job, before I fell asleep. They didn't talk or argue, I just heard drawers opening and closing quietly, and then a couple of clicks that must have been his suitcase. I stared at the dark ceiling, fighting the chest ache. Then my mother said, "You can't just leave without talking to him. You made this mess—you explain it to him."

In the light under my door, I saw the shadow of my father's feet coming. I wished he wouldn't do this. I couldn't face him and didn't want to listen to his speech. I just wanted it to be over.

The door opened. He never wore a shirt at home, but he had one on now.

He closed the door behind him, and we were in the dark again. I couldn't see his face, and that made it easier. "Marc?" he said.

"Uh-huh."

He came and stretched out on my bed next to me, with his shoes on. I could smell that same stale smell he usually had in the morning, before he took his shower.

It took him a while to say anything. Maybe he was afraid I hated him, but I didn't. What he finally said was, "You know your mother and me have been having problems."

"Uh-huh."

"Sometimes two people can't live together. That's just the way it is."

"I know," I said.

"It doesn't have anything to do with you. It's just a problem between her and me. You under-stand that, right?"

"Uh-huh." I picked at some fuzz balls on my blanket.

"We decided we should separate for a while. It's the only thing we can do."

"I know."

"But I'll come see you. We'll spend every Sat-urday together."

His arm felt warm against mine, even through the sleeve. I didn't want him to take it away.

Since I didn't say anything, he asked, "You okay?"

Before my brain knew what the rest of me was doing, I threw my arm over his big belly and said, "I love you, Daddy."

He said, "I love you, too," and squeezed my hand and rubbed it. "I'm sorry about this."

We stayed there like that for a while. I kept being afraid that in the next second he would get up and go, but he didn't, not right away. My arm went up and down with his belly as he breathed.

Finally he let go of my hand. It was time. I rolled back onto my back, and he said, "I'll see you this Saturday."

He sat on the edge of the bed for a moment, and then he stood up. At the door, he said, "You be good, okay?"

"I will."

Then he opened the door and became a dark outline in the light. I wanted to see his face, but he had already turned away.

They didn't talk to each other after that. The front door closed, and I heard my mother lock both locks.

I stayed very still, with my fists under the blanket. Not crying, but fighting down the ache. Every time a car pulled into the little parking lot behind my room, and the headlights swung around and hit my shade, I hoped it was him, and estimated how long it would take for him to walk around to the front and knock on the door and tell my mother, "I'm sorry, it was all my fault, let's try again." But no knocks came.

It took a long time to fall asleep. I didn't really want to—because when I woke up, I wouldn't have a father anymore. Or, that's what it felt like. And how was I going to survive without one?

This is the dream I kept having after he left:

I wake up in the middle of the night and wander into the kitchen. There's my father, just like in the past when I got up at night—eating slices of rye bread and butter at the table while reading the sports page. "Hey, you're supposed to be asleep," he says. I don't mention anything like, "You came back!" because I don't want to mess up the miracle of him being here. He holds my hand, walks me back to my room, and tucks me in. "Okay, champ, see you in the morning," he says, and walks out.

It may not sound like much, but for weeks, every time I climbed into bed, I hoped I would have that dream.

Mr. Vigoritti wrote a note on my homework a couple days later: "Marc, please see me about this." An arrow pointed to one of my answers to a reading question. I read what I had written, and it sounded angry and confused, plus the penmanship was a mess: "Obviously the editors think us kids like to read garbage, or else why would they put such a stupid, unbelievable event into the story?" I couldn't blame him if he said, "Speaking of garbage, how could you hand in such a mixed-up piece of it?"

That's not what he wanted to say to me, though. Instead, he asked, "Is anything going on at home that's bothering you?"

We were standing in the school's side doorway. The rest of the class had already walked out for lunch. He spoke quietly and privately, like no matter what I said, he would understand and keep it to himself.

Across from the school, some boys were wrestling and laughing on the grass. I watched them while I panicked, because even though Mr. Vigoritti would sympathize about my father and Lily, and might even be able to stop the upcoming battle, those things were all Top Secret. Besides, nothing he could do would make Lily like me instead of Nicky. And if he stopped the fight, people would eventually find out it was me who told. And most of all, I didn't want *anyone* to know about my family's problems.

So I made my face innocent and said, "No, nothing's going on."

He said my homework had deteriorated in the past couple days, and he wondered why.

I said, "I just got lazy. I'll try to concentrate more."

He looked closely at me. "You're *sure* you don't want to talk about anything?"

"No. But thanks anyway."

He said, "Words are a powerful thing, Marc. Just talking about what's bothering you can help you feel better. If you decide you'd like to discuss any sort of problem, I'll be happy to listen." He put his hand on my shoulder.

I knew he was trying to help, but all I wanted was to get out of there. I said, "Okay, I'll remember," pulled away from his hand, and hurried home for lunch.

I never did tell him any of my personal problems. But as soon as I was out of his sight, I thought how no one else had ever tried so hard to help me. I wished I could thank him somehow—but, unfortunately, I couldn't do it without giving away my secrets.

· · ·

That afternoon I still couldn't concentrate on my homework. Instead, I took a model of a T-Bird that was all finished except for the paint and put it on the floor, put my atlas on top of it, and stomped on the atlas until the tiny chrome side mirror flew off and the plastic chassis split in two. Then I threw the whole thing in the garbage.

Don't ask why I did it. I can't explain. It just had to be done.

chapter 7

By the time the day of the battle came, our plan seemed insane to me. What was the point of getting our teeth knocked out or our arms broken? Why should thirty guys get hurt just because three or four idiots kept ambushing us? What had seemed like such a matter of honor the week before didn't make any sense at all now.

When you're the underdog, though, you can't say, "Let's talk this over like sensible people," or the other side will say you're weaseling out of it. So no one even mentioned the idea of calling off the fight.

I had on a white shirt and clip-on tie (it was an Assembly day), but I wore my winter coat from last year so it wouldn't matter if it got torn and dirty. Also, I brought my old brown briefcase, from the days before I started tying my books in a red rubber strap. That way, school property wouldn't get wrecked in the fight, and my parents wouldn't get a letter at the end of the year saying they owed the school for new books.

At lunch, Julie Oshinsky came over to me in the playground. I was hanging on to the wire fence by myself, thinking about the fight and my father and Lily, and not having the slightest idea what to do about any of them.

"Hi, Smiley," Julie said.

She had never come over to talk to me before. I had no idea what she wanted.

"Hi," I said.

"Lily told me about the Scrabble game."

Any other time, I would have turned bright red, but right then, I didn't care what she knew.

"I just wanted to tell you, it isn't the end of the world."

"I know."

"You do? Then why do you look like you just got run over by a truck?"

"I have a lot on my mind."

She didn't believe me. She teased me, saying, "Yeah, uh-huh," like I was full of it.

Instead of that annoying me, it made me feel a little better. I guess it was a relief to see *someone* not act all serious.

"Between you and me," she said, "I told Lily she was nuts to like Nicky instead of you. There's no accounting for taste."

I had always liked Julie in general, but I hadn't noticed until then what a terrific person she was.

"What did she say when you said that?"

Julie threw up her hands and her shoulders, making a shrug like a W. "She's crazy, what can I say? She said I didn't understand her."

I searched the playground for Lily and saw her by herself in the far corner, against the fence. She was holding something up to her ear and nodding.

"Is that—?"

"Yeah," Julie answered. "She bought it with her allowance."

I couldn't believe what I was seeing. They would pull you out in a minute for bringing a transistor radio to school—and here came a teacher to grab it from her—but Lily shoved the radio in her coat pocket and hurried away, into the middle of a girls' dodgeball game, and the teacher didn't have the energy to chase after her.

"Looks like our friend is changing," Julie said.

Maybe because she had taken my side with Lily, or just because I needed somebody to talk to, I decided to tell Julie part of what was going on. "I'm not just gloomy about Lily," I said. "We're supposed to have a big fight on Suicide Hill today, us against the guys from 6-309. It's stupid, but there's no way out of it."

"Couldn't you say, 'This is dumb, we're not going to fight'?"

"Not really. We just have to go through with it and do the best we can. Or else they'll call us chicken and beat us up anyway."

"But why can't you explain to them that you're not a bunch of gorillas? If everyone acted like this, the whole world would be at war, people would be punching each other in the street. I can't believe they wouldn't understand."

Although I couldn't imagine making a speech like that, listening to her gave me a tingle in the brain. She had a kind of smartness I had never appreciated before. The things she said all seemed true, but I never would have thought of them by myself. And even though she was an inch taller than me and her ears stuck out of her blond hair a little, she also had sparkly blue eyes that I liked looking into.

The tingly feeling reminded me of the day

when I had first noticed Lily, on the way to our Pizarro report. Would it mean I never cared that much about Lily if I started liking Julie instead?

Maybe. But I hadn't stopped liking Lily, not by a long shot—I just couldn't have her. Anyway, it was too soon to start thinking about someone new, so I just put it off until the future.

The rest of the boys must have had the same grim thoughts as me, because Mr. Vigoritti interrupted his lesson about the form for a Friendly Letter and teased us for looking glum on such a gorgeous, warm day. To wake us up, he took down the pole and pulled some of the tall windows open from the top, letting the fresh air in.

About forty minutes before dismissal, the assistant principal knocked on the window of our classroom door. Mr. Vigoritti went out in the hall to talk to her and told us to begin writing our letters.

We're caught, I thought. Somehow, Mr. Eisenman had found out about the fight and now we would all get pink slips for even planning it. (Did Julie tell?) On the other hand, we wouldn't have to watch our own blood dripping down Suicide Hill.

Someone said in a bad-guy voice, "Okay, who squealed?" Most of the boys let out squashed laughs. When Mr. Vigoritti came back in, though, his face was so dark and sick-looking that we went silent in a split second. He looked like he had to tell us the worst news in the world, and didn't know how to start. All I could think of was that the Russians had dropped an atom bomb on Washington, D.C., and New York was next.

He still had a piece of chalk in his hand from before, but he didn't seem to remember it until he looked down at his fingers. Without saying a word, he turned his back to us and wrote on the board, in his neat script, "Lyndon B. Johnson." When he turned around, he said, "Children— you'll have to learn this name."

Suddenly we heard Mrs. Rothman across the hall burst out crying. He went over and closed the door.

"The president has been shot," he said. "He died a few minutes ago. Lyndon Johnson is the new president of the United States."

I don't think Mr. Vigoritti understood how it could happen any more than I did. If anyone in the world seemed invulnerable, like Superman, it was J. F. K., with his shining smile and twinkling eyes.

No one I knew had ever died before. Not that I *knew* President Kennedy, but I had seen more of him (on TV) than I saw of my aunts and uncles. I didn't have any urge to cry, though—maybe because I couldn't really believe he was dead.

Mr. Vigoritti turned toward the window. No one made a sound, except Phyllis Boberman, who whimpered. I wished that at least one of us could go put an arm around his shoulder, but we were too young.

The picture of J. F. K. above the blackboard, which had looked out over our heads since September, looked sad now—like he was watching over us from the sky, unhappy because he couldn't protect us anymore.

When Mr. Vigoritti faced us, he talked quietly. "Class, I don't know what to say to you. We don't know yet who did it or why. It may turn out to be like other assassinations—Lincoln, Gandhi, even Julius Caesar. Some man or band of men hate the leader of their country, partly because of political beliefs but more because of envy, and work themselves up to a fever pitch . . ."

He stopped talking. We waited for more, but all he said was, "I'm sorry, this isn't helping you. We'll talk about it more when we've calmed down."

He asked us to please observe two minutes of silence for the president, and sat down at his desk, where he leaned his forehead on one hand so his eyes were hidden. We never prayed in my house, but I knew how from TV. I closed my eyes and silently prayed something like this: "God, if you exist, please be good to President Kennedy. He did a lot of great things, like start the Peace Corps and put the astronauts in space. He was so smart, and everybody loved him. And please look out for his wife and children. This must be really terrible for them. (Please don't let anything like this happen to *my* parents. Even if they couldn't get along with each other, at least they're both alive.)"

The two minutes of silence went on longer than my prayer, so I opened my eyes. A breeze from the open window was riffling pages in different people's loose-leaf notebooks. It moved around the room and finally reached my row, the farthest one from the windows. The sheet of paper I was writing my friendly letter on (which said, "Dear Howard, Have you found any interesting rocks or fossils lately?") lifted almost straight up and waved like a flag, then settled down flat again. The breeze made goose pimples on my arms.

Just before three, the principal made a speech over the P.A. system, about how we shouldn't be afraid, because—something about the orderly succession of power and the stability of our government. Whatever he said irritated Mr. Vigoritti. After about a minute, he told us we could ignore the principal's speech and just get ready for dismissal. So Mr. Eisenman's voice kept talking from the speaker while we got our coats and packed up our books and paid no attention to him.

When we got outside, the custodian was lowering the flag to half-staff. I saw my second-grade teacher, Mrs. Frank (who we used to call Mrs. Frankenstein because she was six feet tall and mean), crying in her car. Some crumpled pieces of paper were blowing down the sidewalk, and I got a sick feeling, like the whole country had been torn to pieces. That monk setting himself on fire in Vietnam didn't seem so weird and foreign anymore, because now something awful and insane had happened here, too.

There wasn't time to think about that, though. We had a battle to fight.

The boys from our class met across the street from the school and discussed whether or not we should go through with it, considering what had happened. "Whose idea was this, anyway?" someone asked. I kept my mouth shut.

The guys from 6-309, including Nicky, were already walking up the hill on the other side of the street and looking back at us. So we started walking up, too. It was too warm for my heavy old coat, so I took it off and carried it under my arm.

Cary didn't come with us. We saw him walking uphill toward his house ahead of us, and a couple of his friends called, "Hey, C!" but he ignored them. He had kept to himself all week since the Scrabble game. "I can't believe he would chicken out," someone said, and I answered, "He's not, he just doesn't want any part of it."

Howard gave me a funny look, because what was I doing defending Cary? He didn't know about the Scrabble game and what Cary and I had gone through together.

The main path to the top of the hill went between bushes and boulders. The other guys got to the path first, and we followed them up. I had come down this same trail in the snow dozens of times on my sled. But now, instead of speeding through the clean white snow, we were here to get punched and bloody and to disrespect the death of President Kennedy.

Choosing the top of the hill for the battle was

a big mistake. With all the tangled bushes and the new houses, there was hardly enough room for us all to stand up, let alone fight.

I had always thought of the guys from 6-309 as much bigger than us, but now I noticed that only a few of them were. One kid on their side, with freckles and a plaid tie, had red, wet eyes from crying, and I respected him a lot for caring that much about the president. Nicky kept his hands in his jacket pockets and only looked up from the ground long enough to give me an unhappy glance.

Nobody talked at first. We just looked down at the flat part of Queens, at the junior high school sticking up above all the houses. It was such a clear afternoon, you could see almost to the ocean. You could also see how stupid and wrong this fight was. Unfortunately (I thought), the other class wasn't as wise or mature as me.

One of their guys said, "So, you ready?"

One of us said, "Yeah, what about you?"

"Oh, we're ready."

Joseph acted practical and calm instead of nutty for once. He suggested that since there wasn't enough room to fight all at the same time, we should take turns. Fat Ralph said, "Just don't try to put four of your guys on one of ours, 'cause if you do, then no more rules, we'll slam your heads into the ground."

Howard said, "We're not the ones who gang up on people."

Ralph said, "Okay, one on one, me and you, what are we waiting for?"

Howard looked miserable, but he said, "Fine."

Elliot, who was the tallest one in our class, interrupted. "Hold on a minute," he said to Ralph. "If you want to fight one on one, you can fight me."

"This is between me and him," Ralph said.

"You're just afraid to fight anyone bigger than half your size," Elliot said.

"That's what *you* think."

"That's what I *know.*"

And then, in the middle of all that noise, something unexpected happened. I'm not sure where the nerve came from, to go against the agreed-on plan and risk getting called a coward, but the words exploded out of me: "I don't care what anybody thinks, we shouldn't be doing this. It's a disgrace! The president is dead somewhere, and we're acting like a bunch of animals."

It caught everyone off guard. Finally pimply Ray said, "You're just trying to worm out of—"

But Nicky cut him off. "Shut up. He's right, this is a disgrace."

Matty Parisi, the same guy who tried to steal my Mickey Mantle baseball, said, "We should hold the fight another time, out of respect."

While Ralph and Ray complained about whose side Nicky and Matty were on, I said loudly, "Let's take a vote. Who wants to postpone the fight?"

Nicky and me were the first ones to put up our hands, but in the end every single person raised their hand except Ralph and Ray, who kept muttering about traitors.

Looking at all those guys with their arms up, I couldn't see why we had called them ugly. It was like once the nastiness left their faces, they didn't look any worse than us.

Nicky said, "We should all pray for the president," and recited a short prayer that must have been Catholic, because I couldn't recognize a word of it. While he talked, I thought, He's doing a good thing. He's a decent guy underneath it all. I guess Lily isn't completely out of her mind.

There are a few different paths down from Suicide Hill, depending on which direction you want to go in. The two classes broke into smaller clumps of people, and I walked with Howard down the steep slope that ended by the garages. We didn't talk at all—until we noticed Lily and

Julie down on the sidewalk, turning and walking away fast.

"Look who's here," Howard said, and gave me an elbow in the ribs. He thought she had come to take care of me, when really, she must have been worried about *Nicky* getting hurt. Howard's mistake made my chest ache all over again.

At Howard's corner, we both said, "See you Monday." He stuck out his hand, and I shook it, which was the first and only time we ever did that. When we had gone our separate ways, he called back, "You done good, chum."

By the way, the big fight never happened. Nobody ever mentioned it again. Even Ralph and Ray stopped ambushing us. In the playground after lunch, the two classes just kept to themselves. I considered going up to Nicky and Matty and thanking them for backing me up, but I couldn't think of the right way to put it. We did nod to each other that Monday, though, which meant almost the same thing.

chapter 8

My mother and I watched the president's funeral
on the news a couple days later. We were eating
supper on trays in the living room, like always.
She had managed not to cry in front of me for the
past week, but when J. F. K.'s little son saluted
the casket with the flag over it, that sent her over
the edge. She started sniffling, and then trembling, and then she just gave in and sobbed. It
took me a while to figure out she was crying
about her own problems, not just the president.

She had always called me her "sunshine" and
her "cheerer-upper," so I did my best. I said maybe
we should go to the movies, get out of the house
and have some fun. She calmed herself down and

sniffled, "You're right." Then she gave me one of those Mother looks, full of pride in her young man, etc.—the kind of look that embarrasses you but still feels good.

After she cleaned up her blotchy eye makeup, we walked to the turnpike and saw *Lilies of the Field*. It wasn't my first choice, especially with that title, but the idea was to take *her* mind off her problems, not mine. Through the whole picture, I kept thinking, What a disaster, because it turned out to be in black and white (if we wanted to see black and white, we could've stayed home and watched TV!) and, even worse, the story was about Sidney Poitier helping some German nuns. If you tried for a year, you couldn't have made up a subject that had less to do with us: German nuns! But when the lights came on, she said, "Wasn't that glorious?" So I guess we accomplished our mission, at least.

The point of telling this isn't about the movie, though, it's what happened after. We were walking out past the popcorn stand when my mother said, "That's your old friend Lily, isn't it?"

She was with her mother, coming out through the doors on the other side of the candy stand, gloomy as usual. I didn't want her to see me, especially not with my mother, so I turned my face away. But my social butterfly of a mom called out cheerfully, "Jeanette?"

Mrs. Wu didn't recognize my mother until she saw me. Then she smiled and pulled Lily over to us. "Hello, Sybil," she said. "Hello, Marc." She put her hand on her daughter's shoulder, and Lily peeped, "Hi."

I can't remember their small talk, but when Mrs. Wu asked how my father was—just an innocent question, I don't think she had ever met him—my mother said, "We've separated," acting matter-of-fact about it. And then, as if her announcing the news to the world wasn't bad enough, when Mrs. Wu said, "Oh, I'm sorry," my mother fell apart again.

I couldn't stand for Lily to see her crying. So, while Mrs. Wu touched Mom's arm and said, "It must be so hard," I said to Lily, "Come over here," and led her to the wall with posters for coming attractions.

We hadn't stood this close to each other since the Scrabble game. There was a tall metal ashtray between us, full of sand and cigarette butts, and I kept staring into it. Neither one of us wanted to be there, but since we had no choice, somebody had to say something.

I asked if she liked the movie. She said it was

all right. Then she said, "I'm sorry about your parents."

"It's probably for the best."

"Why? What do you mean?"

"They couldn't live together. At least now I don't have to listen to them fight."

Even if I sounded phony, acting tough about it helped me talk to her, so I kept it up. "I saw you at Suicide Hill the other day," I boldly mentioned.

She clenched up in embarrassment.

"You came to take care of Nicky if he got hurt, right?"

"I didn't know what to do. Julie said we shouldn't let you boys go through it alone. But I thought . . . I was worried that you and Cary might beat him up."

I laughed in a sarcastic sort of way.

"Why are you laughing?" she asked.

"*Us,* beat up *Nicky?* Right—when Niagara Falls."

"You talk about him like he's some kind of killer. He's not a criminal."

"I know. He's all right. He's just completely wrong for you."

I couldn't believe I had come right out and said it! Now she would really attack me. I stared at some butts with red lipstick rings in the ash-tray, and waited for a tongue-lashing.

But she just said, "Everyone thinks I'm a certain way. They're wrong."

"Yeah, what are you really, a Communist spy?"

"I don't *want* to be quiet and studious. I'm sick of it! I want to be more like Nicky."

I pretended that what she said didn't surprise me, or bother me. "Like how? What do you want to do, start punching people?"

She peeked over at her mother, to make sure she couldn't hear. "I hate being so polite and obedient all the time. I'd like to do things no one would expect me to do—like wear makeup, or curse out loud. Just, to not always be boring and nice."

Makeup. Cursing.

Believe it or not, hearing those words helped me. At least now I knew what she was thinking, and why she looked unhappy, and why she would never want to go out with me.

Afterward, I thought that maybe I should have acted heroic and advised her to tell Nicky how she felt, on the off chance he might feel the same way. But I didn't have it in me—then, or ever.

When our mothers came over to us, mine had

messed up her eye makeup again, but she was smiling and wiping her face with a Kleenex. "We're going to walk home together," she told me.

And that's what we did. Our mothers walked behind us, while Lily and I moved on to less painful subjects. When we passed the barbershop, I told her about the time I got mad at the barber because he pushed my head down too hard, and when he gave me bubble gum at the cash register, I threw it down on the floor. She told how she once bought a green turtle at Woolworth's for twenty-nine cents, and then it died the same night. It turned out we both used to hate going to the grocery store because the crowds of women pushing shopping carts never noticed us down below and rammed into us. And she reminded me about something I had forgotten, from her birthday party at the Hamburger Coach: how I helped her father stand up a bunch of mah-jongg tiles on a table, which he knocked over like dominoes so they formed the word LILY, in script.

We were just little kids in all of these stories, but now we had grown up. Here I was, strolling with Lily down the turnpike, talking like old friends. It was almost exactly what I had wished for since the day of our Pizarro report. And even though we weren't holding hands, it felt good just to be with her and hear about her memories—and finally just to *talk* to her again.

chapter 9:
afterward

My mother took driving lessons and passed her test, and my father gave her the Rambler. He bought a used Plymouth Valiant for himself, and he's been picking me up every Saturday, like he promised, at eleven o'clock.

The way it works is, I come up with an idea for something to do, and as long as it's not too expensive, he'll do it with me. So far we've gone to a batting range, played miniature golf, watched jets take off at the airport, and took the Day Line up the Hudson River to Bear Mountain. Sometimes we just practice baseball like before. He pitches to me, then hits me grounders and line drives that I have to dive for. He's a lot nicer about it now—like, if I duck away from a hard grounder that bounced up at my face, instead of yelling, "What are you, ball-shy?" now he'll say, "We'd better work on those reflexes."

I'd say we talk more these days than we used to when he lived at home. He tells me stories while we drive, like about when he was a kid in Brooklyn, how he used to explore the tunnels of the new subway lines with his friends before they put the tracks in. Those are my favorite times, just riding around in the car with him and hearing about him as a boy.

He's even polite to my mother. When he knocks on the door, instead of grunting or calling her names, he asks, "How are you doing?" He still hasn't mentioned his girlfriend to me, and to tell the truth, I'm glad, because it's hard enough knowing he has one without hearing all the details. When he brings it up, I'll face up to it then.

(I guess I should be grateful to her—whoever she is; she's the one who cured him of being angry all the time. And actually, even though it hurts that our family broke apart, I wouldn't go back to the way it was before for a million bucks.)

One hot Saturday just after school ended for

the year, we went to the World's Fair and I spot-ted Mr. Vigoritti on a line. He was with two older ladies, who turned out to be his mother and his sister. I pointed him out to my father—quietly, because it's always weird to meet a teacher outside school—but my father led me right over and said, "Mr. Vigoritti?" (My old father, the grouchy one who used to live with us, never would have done that. He would've said, "Hm," and kept walking.)

Mr. Vigoritti didn't have on his usual gray suit and tie, just a sports jacket and a white shirt. When he shook hands with my father, it gave me a strange tingle, like they belonged in different universes and weren't ever supposed to meet.

My father said, "I want to thank you. From what Marc says, I can tell you did a tremendous job. He never got such good grades before."

Although I probably turned the color of a tomato, I didn't mind him saying it, because I wanted Mr. Vigoritti to know what a great teacher he was.

He replied, "The pleasure was all mine." He told his sister and mother, "We had a playwriting competition at the end of the year, and Marc won. He wrote about a boy who's held prisoner by a band of terrifying monsters. But a bird teaches him to fly, and he escapes by diving right out the tower window." (I didn't mention my play before because I wrote it in May, after all these other stories happened.)

"Sounds pretty original," his sister said.

Mr. Vigoritti stared down at the ground for a minute, then looked up and said, "I'd like to give you something." From inside his jacket he took out the black and gold fountain pen he always wrote with. "You'll recognize the ink from your homework. Think of it as my contribution to your career as a playwright."

I couldn't believe he would give me that pen. All I could think of to say was, "Thank you." I just hoped he understood that it meant more to me than I knew how to show.

"That's some gift," my father said when we were by ourselves. I unscrewed the cap so we could look at the gold tip. It was a thick and heavy kind of pen, heavier than about six of my Bics put together. I knew immediately that I would only use it to write things that were special and important.

Later that day, we went to see the Time Capsule at the Westinghouse Pavilion. That was when I figured out what to write with Mr. Vigoritti's pen.

The Time Capsule is an indestructible torpedo

filled with things like a flag, a Bible, a bikini, and credit cards. They're planning to bury it for a hundred years so people in 2064 can get a better idea of what it's like to live right now. Seeing it got me thinking about what *I'd* like to save forever. At first all I could think of was the ball with Mickey Mantle's autograph, and Mr. Vigoritti's fountain pen. Then I thought, No, even more than those things, I would want to save my memories of sixth grade—of Lily and Howard and Nicky and Julie—of the petrified rock, and the fights, and the Scrabble game, and Mr. Vigoritti's stories about J. F. K.

And so, starting that night, I've been writing this story of 6-321.

We were supposed to put on *Julius Caesar* just before Christmas break, but the principal wanted to cancel it because he said it would be in poor taste to show an assassination onstage after the president's death. The whole class got extremely upset about it—all that memorizing, down the drain!—especially Nicky, but Mr. Vigoritti convinced the principal that, if we gave a little talk beforehand, the play would have extra meaning for all the students in the school. When he came back and told us the show would go on, we yelled, "Hip hip hooray!"

My mother said afterward that the production was fabulous. After exaggerating how wonderful I was, she mentioned that the boy who played Caesar had real charisma.

School never got easy for Nicky, but he didn't seem to care. And starting before Christmas, he had a girlfriend: Lily. They tried to keep it secret, probably so Lily's parents wouldn't forbid her to see him, but they didn't try hard enough, because one afternoon I saw them holding hands outside Woolworth's. He was singing a song with his free hand out like Frank Sinatra, and she had on eye makeup and was laughing. I ducked into the bagel store and stayed hidden until they went by.

In all our years of school, I had never seen her as happy as then. She looked like a teenager on a date with a movie star. I'll admit it made me jealous and unhappy again for a day or two—but it didn't hurt as much as it could have, because I had a new friend of my own by then. Julie and I went from doing things in groups (like the snowy day when six of us played with her Ouija board in her room) to just her and me doing homework together, to me whispering jokes from the row behind her in the auditorium, the day before Christmas vacation, when they showed us the TV opera *Amahl and the Night Visitors.* (Mr. Eisenman pulled me out for that, a big yank on the shoulder, but his evil eye didn't scare me anymore, and when I told my mother what the pink slip was for, she called him a little dictator.)

It's not exactly a romance, but we have fun whenever we're together. Like, walking down the turnpike once, we started singing, "She loves you, yeah, yeah, yeah," out of nowhere, and went, "WOOOOO!" and shook our heads like the Beatles. And then, when her parents went out for their anniversary, she came over and ate franks and beans with my mother and me, and we all started cracking each other up. "Who makes the best franks and beans?" my mother asked, and I said, "Dr. Frank N. Bean," and Julie said, "No, it's Judge Felix Frankfurter."

My mother laughed with her old horse whinny, a way she hadn't laughed in a long, long time. We kept going with more hot dog jokes, and she even came up with one herself: "He's the wiener, and still champion!"

So that's another good thing about Julie—she helped my mother remember how to have a good time and be silly.

The only awkward moment Julie and I ever

had came when she admitted she was the one who had told Nicky about Lily liking him. I knew she had meant it as a good deed, since she was Lily's friend, but it still bothered me.

I got over it by the next day, though. We went to Woolworth's and took funny pictures together in the photo booth, clowning in different ways for each shot. Afterward, we cut the strip in half so we each got two pictures, and I taped mine to the wall over my desk. Now I can look up from my homework anytime and laugh at her cross-eyes and my dastardly villain eyebrows.

One snowy afternoon, Cary came up to me after school. He just started walking alongside me and said, "I guess you know about Lily and Nicky."

They had been going out for months, but he must have only heard about it then.

I shrugged and said, "She's not exactly like we thought she was."

He didn't agree or disagree, but he stunned me by saying, "I wanted to apologize for the way I acted with you."

"No sweat," I said.

And that was that. He turned around and walked home with his head down.

Not that I wish he would turn back into his old nasty jerk self, but I hope his spirits pick up again soon. You don't want to see even your old enemy *that* depressed.

On Christmas Day I went into the city with Howard and Joseph and Elliot—the first time my mother let me go in without her. It was my idea, to have an adventure all by ourselves. We took the bus and then the subway to Rockefeller Center, where we watched the skaters and the giant tree and looked at the fancy store windows. Then we ate supper at the Automat and went to see *Soldier in the Rain,* with Jackie Gleason and Steve McQueen, because *It's a Mad Mad Mad Mad World* wasn't playing anymore. It turned out to be a pretty weird movie, but we laughed a lot anyway. (The best part was the soda machine that only Jackie Gleason could slap just right so it gave him a free bottle of Pepsi.)

After the movie we marched through Times Square with our arms hooked together, singing the marching song from the movie, "I don't know but I've been told . . . Eskimo girls are mighty cold." We must have looked pretty dumb, but it felt great to be in the city alone, like army buddies on a one-day pass, with the huge buildings lit up above us, and the sky as dark as purple ink, and each of us making some joke that was stupider than the last one (but that we all laughed at anyway). We still had half of sixth grade to get through, but going to the city made us feel adult and independent. Now that we were older, we could do things like this more often: go out and act crazy if we wanted to, without parents or teachers there to make us be quiet.

That's the best part about growing up—you get to be free.

About the Story

Turning the aches and triumphs of childhood into a story more than thirty years after the fact turned out to be a more complicated task than I had expected.

I've wanted to write about the sixth grade for a long time, because the memories mean so much to me. This was the turning point in my life: the moment when a demanding teacher encouraged me and I began to care about doing well in school. There were so many stories to tell, I didn't know where to start. Sitting down with my class picture one night, I typed everything I could remembered about each person, including

their talents, their
oked like.

ories in, I wrote
e around, with
hirty-one stu-
gh, that I had
not all of it was
, cutting out whole subplots
oping other parts of the story more
fully.

In the course of rewriting the book, I decided
to replace certain true, but dull, details with
more interesting fictions. For example, the sweet
girl I had a crush on in sixth grade was Jewish,
like almost everyone else in my neighborhood; I
made her Chinese.

For me, one of the most important parts of
6-321 is the narrator's voice. In order to make
Marc Chaikin sound real, I went back to papers
I'd saved from sixth grade: homework assign-
ments, school newspaper articles, and my scrapbook. Marc's storytelling doesn't sound quite as
clumsy as my own writing at his age, but I did
use certain phrases that popped up repeatedly. (In
my scrapbook, especially, I affected a lofty disdain
for everything, and described whatever I didn't
admire as *garbage*.)

Finally, you wouldn't think that writing your own history requires research, but I did, in fact, spend many hours in the library, taking notes on which news stories happened when, and what ads were out that year, and even what topics were covered in the New York City curricula for sixth grade. All of these pieces of information stirred up memories and enriched the story. And, really, it was *fun* to dive back into the past that way, and to discover that, in every issue of *Time* magazine, there were news events that I vividly remembered.

The simple point of all this is that much more goes into telling an autobiographical story than it may seem. What you end up with after all the revision and research may no longer be a true history—but it's a better story.

—M. L.